PRAKASH BAL JOSHI is a multifaceted personality with four decades in journalism, creative writing and international recognition as an artist. He has four books to his credit: Prakash *Bal Joshi Yanchya Katha* (Prakash Bal Joshi's Stories) and *Maitrinichi Goshta* (Story of a Friend) – both collections of short stories, while Gateway explores the complexities and contradictions of urban life in Mumbai, accompanied by sketches, and *Poll Book 2000*.

He has held several solo and group shows of his paintings: oil on canvas, in India as well as in Bressuire in France, Chicago, Las Vegas and Minneapolis in the USA, Basel (Switzerland), Lisbon (Portugal), Moscow (USSR), Osijek (Croatia) and other centres in Europe, Izmir (Turkey), and Thimphu (Bhutan). His art installation, 'God's Particle', at the India Art Festival, Mumbai 2012, received international appreciation as scientists working on this experiment got the Nobel Prize in 2013. He was selected as ethics adviser by World Citizen Artists, an international artists' group. He was appointed a jury member for an international art competition organized in London at Belgravia Art Gallery in Mayfair, an international art hub.

A veteran Mumbai-based journalist, Prakash has worked with several national publications including The Times of India. He was chairman of the Mumbai Union of Journalists. (*website: www. prakashbaljoshi.com*)

SMITA KARANDIKAR is a lecturer of English in a junior college; this is her first work of translation.

This collection of fifteen short stories by Prakash Bal Joshi explores contemporary themes revolving around strained relationships, changing values and women empowerment among middle-class people in both rural and urban settings. What makes these narratives remarkably distinct is the sensitive, at times disturbing yet humane, portrayal of the characters, each going through his/her unique set of trials and tribulations in life without any value judgement by the author, leaving the readers to contemplate and draw their own interpretations. Each story has a sketch by the author which depicts his visualization – restless, illusionary, incomprehensible – lending a rather mysterious touch to his narratives.

All through his career spanning four decades, Joshi has donned multiple hats of being a poet, writer, painter, social worker, while primarily being a journalist, columnist and political reviewer. Originally written in Marathi, these stories capture in English translation the struggles and conflicts in our ever-changing society with a fluidity that resonates in the hearts of its audience long after they have experienced it.

RATNA TRANSLATION SERIES

MIRROR IN THE HALL

AND OTHER STORIES

PRAKASH BAL JOSHI

TRANSLATED FROM MARATHI BY
SMITA KARANDIKAR

RATNA BOOKS

Original Marathi copyright © Prakash Bal Joshi 2015

First Published in English Translation 2019
English Translation copyright © Prakash Bal Joshi 2019

Cover and endpaper paintings & text illustrations copyright
© Prakash Bal Joshi 2019

ISBN   978-93-5290-740-3 (POD)

Published by **RATNA BOOKS**
An imprint of Ratna Sagar P. Ltd.
Virat Bhavan, Mukherjee Nagar Commercial Complex
Delhi 110009, India
www.ratnabooks.in

Contents

1. Mirror in the Hall	1
2. Short-term Memory Loss	7
3. Raatraani	17
4. Molestation	33
5. Dissection	61
6. Just Two Words	73
7. Four Zeros	89
8. Box of Sweets	105
9. Dad and the Interview	113
10. The Bridge	121
11. Deshmukh	133
12. Amolik	155
13. Need to Visit	173
14. Bus Ticket	187
15. Speaking with Sparrows	203

Mirror in the Hall

As soon as I was born, the haze-like reddish darkness faded and my eyes opened into a void where no light entered. I could only feel an emptiness encircling and sheathing me.

I went on peering into the void until blank sight was replaced by an unknown sensation. I felt someone thumping my back. Suddenly, all sorts of strange noises, feeble as well as loud, attacked my consciousness. As shadows began swirling around me and unknown odours assaulted my senses, the warm and much familiar smell receded and retreated into the recent, yet unfamiliar past.

1

I saw her. She was in all white, but the jet black eyes made a contrast. The startling whiteness was unsettling and frightened me, but the dark eyes held me in a spell. Their whirlpool depths bewitched and transfixed me into submission.

I could feel her but she seemed unaware of my fresh consciousness. She went on patting my back, thumping me, swaying me back and forth, and looking at me with great concern. The darkness of her eyes was filled with worry.

'Sister,' somebody bellowed. She hurriedly opened her purse and her slender fingers moved about so quickly and delicately that I was mesmerized. She slipped out a small mirror from her purse, as if easing a baby from a recalcitrant womb.

She wanted me to look at myself before I looked out at the unknown world. But before she could place the mirror before my face, I had already discovered myself. Her jet black eyes were so clear and reflective that I had seen myself as well as my identification badge. Unaware of my discovery, she went on polishing the mirror and soon after the mirror was clear enough, she held it in front of me. I was still captivated by the darkness of her eyes and realizing that I was not looking at the mirror, she whispered, 'Look, have a look, before you see anything else.'

I could barely understand her. What I saw was the image of a premature infant about a minute old, with embryonic liquid still clinging onto a pink, feather-soft face. This image looked down possessively at me from the mirror.

Satisfied, she slowly put me down. My eyes clung to her as she rummaged through her purse again, fished out a thick pencil, held the mirror in front of her face and applied the pencil onto her rather conspicuous lips. The lips started glowing red.

Quickly, she lowered her face. Now her lips were more prominent than her eyes and she planted a hurried kiss on my cheek. I started crying, for the first time I think.

My crying was terrifying even to myself. It was completely different from the noises that I had been accustomed to. A reassuring pat fell on my back. It was my mother, trying to calm me, but I went on bawling because I wanted to listen to this new exciting sound. This went on till some new presence came up to me.

I WAS STARTLED BY WHITENESS, though of a different kind. Mother said he was my father. Daddy had a strong broad face, with a bluish tinge in his eyes. Bushy eyebrows gave him a fearsome look. He wore a white dhoti, white full-sleeved shirt and white cap, representative of the nation's freedom struggle. The cap, I was to learn later, also ensured a quick ascent on the power ladder after Independence.

His obsession with white was all pervasive. Except for his eyes and dark bushy eyebrows, he was a white man. His stern look stopped my howling. He winked and smiled a typical half-smile, which failed to arouse any confidence in me, and I continued sobbing.

A black crow, settled on the branch of a peepal tree, was

visible from where I was lying. It suddenly opened its long beak and crowed loudly. I started howling again. My father dashed to the window and closed it with a bang. My mother tried to calm me down and asked my father to open the window. He refused to do so. How could he allow his son to look at a black crow, the bearer of bad tidings? Moreover, it was totally black opposed to his sense of pristine whiteness.

It was a huge mansion with many rooms and a spacious hall. My father, a busy and influential man, would often meet visitors at the entrance. He would allow visitors to enter the hall only after they had washed their hands and feet at the entrance. All this trouble, I was told, was for the sake of a large mirror, a family heirloom, which had been handed down for at least four generations, and father wanted to keep it absolutely clean and pure.

Often he would peep inside, while discussing serious matters with visitors just to find out what I was up to. He would repeatedly say, 'Go and wash your hands, they are dirty. Look at your feet, go wash them first.' These instructions would be repeated like a litany every day.

Let me see your hands, wash them first.
Let me see your hands, well.
Let me see your feet, wash them first.
Let me see your feet, good.
Wash your hands, wash your feet.
Wash your face, good.

My mother's task was to keep a strict watch on me. I should not play with urchins; I should not play with clay or I would

4

become dirty. I used to wonder how he kept himself so clean despite meeting so many dirty fellows every day in the hall.

I could not understand why I was not allowed to play. What if my hands and feet got dirty? I could always wash them before I entered the hall so that the family mirror remained uncontaminated. How could I not touch and play with mother earth? I desperately wanted to mould clay into beautiful images and idols. But I dared not, not with my father anxiously hovering about in the background.

The commandments of 'thou shalt not' became too much to bear. One day I simply went out, used the water meant for washing one's hands and feet for softening clay, and clumsily began making various idols.

When I returned home, my mother was sitting in a corner, her forehead clean as a slate. She did not say a word about my dirty hands and feet. I did not notice that there was no kumkum on her forehead.

I looked at the mirror in the hall. It was cracked, as if somebody had thrown a stone at it. My face was also divided along the lines of the splintered glass surface. Suddenly, I realized why the mirror had cracked.

I had been telling him not to try and enter the mirror. How could one wash images? In the far corner of the mirror, I could see bits and pieces of forms I had created from mud.

Short-term Memory Loss

S HE CROSSED THE ROAD IN A HURRY, weaving through vehicles that slowed down as the signal turned red, and reached the opposite side of the road. Stepping on to the tiled footpath, she hesitated, not knowing whether to turn right or left. Looming over her was a huge cut-out of Salman Khan, winking and pointing a finger at her. Her attention swivelled from his bare chest to the earring on his left ear till she was abruptly shoved ahead by an impatient crowd as the signal turned green.

Aimlessly, she walked towards a huge window, trying to recollect why she had, in the first place, crossed the road away from the footpath leading to Churchgate railway station.

Preoccupied with her own thoughts, she walked carelessly towards 'Talk of the Town', an open-air restaurant frequented mostly by foreigners, crossed the Marine Drive and sat down on the wall overlooking the Arabian Sea. It was hot and sultry, but she was overwhelmed by the sea breeze carrying the odour of rotten seaweed. She felt frightened of the waves breaking on the wave breakers below the wall on which she was sitting. She wanted to run back home and hug Deepak.

SHE WAS CONFUSED and did not know why he was talking incessantly about his childhood days. And amazed at the way he could recollect minute details of his early years. Was he still obsessed with his childhood? Maybe, but she was not interested. It was too much to listen to him meander through places and people who were distant not only from her, but from him as well. The only early childhood memory she could remember was her mother's strident admonitions. She would reflexively lift up a corner of her lace-frock waist high with her right hand and put it in her mouth while reciting poems to strangers gathered in a dimly lit dining room. She would often do this when singing 'Baa baa black sheep…have you any wool?'

She could still feel the stern look on her father's face as she lifted up her frock. She would freeze and forget the next lines of the poem. With the upraised frock in her hand, her father's stern look and her mother's shrill shouts to put her frock down, she could hardly go beyond 'baa baa black sheep…'

Visitors would sympathize with her plight. She could clearly recall that she would hate her parents and like the visitors' sympathy and the reassuring and comforting pats on her back.

She had some hazy memories of going to school, but there was nothing very distinct or special about her early days. She would often wonder why Deepak talked about his childhood so much. Was he showing off or was he still a growing child?

Perhaps showing off was a sign of not growing up? She was confused and could not decide what the reason was behind his ceaseless chatter. Not that she could ever recall what he said, but his lip movements were etched in her mind. And when he edged closer in a romantic mood, she would stare at his lips, hoping that they would still keep moving; instead, they would move closer to her lips. Looking at her watch, she became anxious. It was almost 12:30 p.m. and Deepak had not returned. She put the book on a side table, switched off the reading light and gazed out of the small window. She was trying to recollect the last time his lips had come close, but she could not – she felt frightened.

THE EARLY MORNING RUSH renders her immobile as commuters from behind push her sideways and march ahead. She is rather slow compared to them. Making a mental check of what she has to do today, she peers at the thronging crowd – a huge millipede moving in one direction with its numerous feet…Catches a glimpse of a familiar face, but she is not sure whether she knows him, so she turns away from the face which she has recognized. The commuter notices her and smiles warmly. She hesitatingly smiles back, but keeps moving ahead as she does not want to miss her regular train. The face, caught in the maze of moving heads, moves towards her from the opposite direction, blocks her path and says 'hello'. She has to move aside so that other commuters can pass by her.

'How is Deepak? Do you recognize me?' he asks, noticing her uncertain expression. Her 'yes' is so feeble and inaudible that it actually means no, but he ignores her response. 'Sorry to disturb you like this, but did you get the number I wanted?' he asks. The question, coming out of the blue, flabbergasts her. She just does not know what he is talking about. Now she starts perspiring and she knows the reason. It is not embarrassment but the realization that some unknown monster is eating you up.

Seeing a question mark, he tries to explain, 'Remember we met last week and Deepak was saying you know some family doctor who is good and reliable...' he continues talking.

She knows the doctor in the locality who she thinks is good, but she does not remember meeting this guy with Deepak last week. She is about to say, 'Where did we meet?' but she hesitates and swallows her words. She fumbles for her telephone diary and gives up.

'Sorry, I don't have it right now. I'll give it to you later. Will that do? And I've to rush now, is it okay?'

'Okay, see you some time. I stay a little way off from your building. We will catch up with each other later. Bye.' He vanishes in the crowd.

She closes her purse lest something fall out of it as she is being jostled around. She joins the stream of commuters flowing towards platform number two – for the train taking her to CST – the last suburban station in the central business district of Mumbai.

She clambers onto the train. It is almost full, and she gets the fourth seat, very uncomfortable. She squeezes in somehow. She soon forgets about the unknown face and the fact that she had forgotten meeting him with Deepak last week.

She sees Rosy jumping in from the door just before the trains start moving in. She is such an exuberant person. 'Hi Rosy! Nice dress. New one?' she asks, waving at her. Rosy comes near her, 'Are you kidding? It is new but you commented on it the day before yesterday.' Rosy starts rambling about other topics, but her remark pierced through her head like a hot iron pin.

Rosy's bright blue dress with a yellow design remained in her mind even when immersed in the daily grind of office work. She, however, has no time to brood on the puzzling question as to how she could forget about the new dress about which she had already commented. How could she?

There is no time to think about such trivia. When did she meet that guy she bumped into at the railway station this morning? Okay, cool down, it does not matter. People keep forgetting things and there is nothing to worry about, she keeps telling herself as she quickly swallows her lunch at the office canteen with her regular office group. They are discussing the merits and demerits of the latest Bollywood movie.

As she leaves the office and starts walking towards Churchgate, she clutches her purse as she feels the sea wind blowing over her. She has forgotten about the unknown face she had encountered and Rosy and her frock, but she is gripped with a new worry – the man at the station had reminded her of a more important thing which she had forgotten over the last couple of days. Or was she trying to avoid the matter?

Her family doctor. She must go and meet him immediately. She just cannot afford to delay anymore. This time she has not mentioned it to Deepak.

He is always angry and irritable. She decided not to confide in him as he would again lose his temper. She is not sure whether she took the pill last night. Yes or no, maybe yes or maybe no…'You cannot be so unsure,' he barks at her.

All the romance and pleasure snatched out of a hectic weekly schedule has gone out of his as well as her consciousness. 'You bloody well fuck the shit out of me every time you use the excuse of forgetfulness. You do not know whether you took the fucking pill or not. You are not sure. What do we do now?' he keeps ranting.

She clutches her head every time he starts shouting. 'Do you think we can afford a kid at this time? You and I both have to work. How else can we pay for this fucking flat? Do I have to repeat myself again and again? How can you not remember if you took the pill or forgot to take it…tomorrow you will forget who I am…?'

'Stop it, for god's sake. Stop it. I wish I had not told you about it.' Her head reeling, she rushes to the washbasin to vomit.

This has been happening on and off. They tried using some other form of contraception and gave up as both found them unacceptable.

'How can you forget about pills?' asked her mother in disbelief when she confided in her. 'Don't blame him. It is your mistake. How can you forget, or forget to remember?'

'It's not only the pill, mom, to tell you the truth; I keep forgetting almost everything…I'm afraid.' Almost in tears, she tries to hide her face from her mother.

SHE HURRIES TOWARDS the station. She must call on the doctor and tell him. Actually, she has forgotten when they had sex the last time and she is not sure whether she had taken the pill or not. She cannot afford to ignore or delay seeing the doctor. And Deepak is also not aware that he is complicating things. While walking, she takes out a water bottle from her carry bag and keeps gulping till the last drop, closes the cover and shoves the bottle back into the bag.

With drops of water still lingering on her face, she feels the cool breeze brushing her face and running through the thick hair falling across her eyes. She pushes the hair back behind her long ears. Her uncle used to smile at the extraordinary long ears and compliment her for being intelligent, like an elephant. She smiles nostalgically.

Instead of crossing the road to enter the station and take the train back home, she starts walking towards the seashore. As she comes near a signal, it turns green and she is pushed by the homeward-bound crowd into walking towards the station and she keeps on walking, forgetting her earlier desire to spend some time at the seashore.

All along her return journey from her workplace, she broods over her memory loss. It is not that she does not remember things. She does remember complicated things, projects, deadlines and telephone numbers, but trivial matters bother her the most...she does not know what she will suddenly forget. And it really scares her. It is turning dark and as she gets out of the train, she walks first to her flat to change and then she will go to the clinic, a small visiting room where the doctor is visible, waiting for patients.

She turns on the lights as she enters the flat on the tenth floor. It is turning dark and sultry. She takes out a glass of chilled water from the fridge and gulps it down. Before taking a shower and changing, she takes a look at the PC. It is sitting dead on the desk in the corner. While taking a shower, she takes a look at her tummy – is it looking bloated? Suddenly, she remembers to check a mail from the company where she had applied for a better job providing better terms.

She turns on the PC, looks into the mirror and hastily clambers into her clothes. By then, the PC is fully booted...She types in her login name, Priya.patelxyz@gmail.com, enters her password and waits for the page to come alive. It returns, saying that either the log-in name or the password was wrong, and that she should check her log-in name or password.

She does it again and the same page returns without taking much time, asking her once again to check her log-in name and password. Now she is scared. Have I forgotten the log-in name or the password? I have been using this email day in and out; how can I forget my log-in name or password. Next, it says that the password is case-sensitive.

Even though she has taken a bath and is sitting below a fan, beads of sweat start collecting on her forehead. She is scared and frightened. No longer does she think of unknown or strange faces, Rosy's frock, the seashore and the family doctor, or for that matter, Deepak. She does not feel the urge to go back into Deepak's arms to seek comfort anymore.

She becomes uneasy as even her mother's features turn hazy as she mentally chants 'baby don't worry, everything will be alright'. She looks down from the window at the vehicular traffic below, forgetting that she is looking down from the tenth floor.

She suddenly feels attracted to the moving red lights below, drawing a sort of fading red line on a wet tar road…

Raatraani

SITTING ON THE CHAIR, close to the window, she is looking
out. Rains have just stopped. A wisp of a cloud is hovering
near the hill. Otherwise, the sky is clear blue. Just behind
the hill, at the foot of the mountains, torrential winds are
convulsively shaking and rocking the thick trees left and right.
It seemed as if a wild animal is making desperate and frantic
efforts to get free; it gets weary and tired, waits for some time,
crouching and then springs back again with renewed energy.

Apart from the ticking of the clock, she could hear the
rustling of the leaves. 'This sound of the leaves playing
arrogantly with the winds – is it really audible? Or is it a

17

hallucination?' She is forever hounded by these questions. Once casually she told him, 'How very pleasant is the sound of the leaves! Isn't it?'

'Which leaves?' he had asked her.

Through the window, the forest that was lush green in the rains looked arid in the winter. The winding highway and the hill itself were absolutely barren. Behind the hill are the mountain ranges and at its foot are the newly planted cypress trees.

'Those ones, at the foot of the mountains.'

'Which ones? You mean those ones? Oh dear, they look as if they are close. But do you know how far they are? How is it possible to hear the rustling of those leaves sitting right over here?'

'I can hear them.'

'It might be audible to you but sadly I don't have long ears like you!' he joked.

She was hurt.

She remembered she had read somewhere that some people are highly sensitive and, compared to others, more receptive. Even though that explained the fact, she was hurt by the manner in which he had scornfully said that he was unable to hear. Not just that. He also hinted that it was impossible for her also to hear it. 'Is my hearing a reality or his saying that it must be an illusion correct?' – A spine-chilling thought. She wrapped her shawl tighter around her.

'With whom should I check whether the sound is really audible or not? Hardly anyone visits this secluded government bungalow on the outskirts of the village. The maid comes but she never lifts up her head nor does she talk. She must be half deaf because one has to instruct her loudly to get things done. She comes, washes utensils and clothes, sweeps and mops without uttering a single word and then leaves.'

Many a time she has watched the movements of the trees so intently and minutely, that even their slightest movement gets imprinted on her mind.

Sometimes the postman visits. He rings the bell, drops the mail in the box and leaves in such a hurry that by the time one goes out to open the door, he has already closed the gate behind him and left.

Letters were the only entertainment. Earlier, there used to be regular exchanges of letters. She used to write with enthusiasm. But gradually that also subsided. 'What and how much to write? Apart from the same old topics like the lush green mountains, trees, goats and sheep, the occasional sighting of wild animals, the unknown local language and festivals, shopping – what else to write? And that too again and again!' She realized that monotony had started seeping in. 'Days too are similar. What can be done?' Saying so, she stopped writing letters.

On her own, she never again broached the topic of the leaves, but it was always lurking nearby. One fine day he happened to ask, 'What's so attractive about the trees that you keep watching them?' Known otherwise for being calm and quiet, she lost her cool that day. 'What do you mean? I just like looking at the trees. That's all. What else do I have to see and watch here?'

He regretted asking the question. It was as if the accumulated water of many years had gushed out with a strong current.

'You have thrown me into this jungle, cut me off from my relatives. What else is there to do here? No entertainment, no plays nor any movies. No one to talk to. You go for your job. I sit here like a ghost, watching the trees. If you don't want me to do so, at least let me know what I should do?' Words flowed out in a rush.

When she first came here, her mother had accompanied her. She used to feel afraid being alone. But after some days, she got habituated. His colleagues told them that everything was safe and there was nothing to be afraid of.

The village had about four to five hundred locals. On the outskirts were some ten to twelve living quarters for the government officials. It would take a five-hour journey to reach the district headquarters and two days to reach Mumbai. Newspaper reached after a day. Even if it had reached the same day, what would be the use? There was absolute stillness and total silence throughout. Since the bungalow was at the posterior side and on a higher plinth, the houses in the neighbourhood also were not visible. The only movement seen was of the cars on the highway which was visible in the distance. During the day, ten to twelve trucks, four or five government cars and jeeps, and a single bus passed by. A bizarre calm surrounded the bungalow.

Sometimes children from the neighbouring areas came to

play in the open ground, and there was some liveliness. After a few games, they would come to the gate asking for water to drink. A jug full of water with two glasses was more than sufficient. They would gulp it down and run away. What and how to talk with them? While going back, someone would say 'bye'. That's all.

After the evening tea, she is usually in the veranda, pacing up and down; gazing at the hill in front, the trees behind it, the mountain range touching the blue sky. The sun sets here quite early. Finishing the day's work, he comes home by five, five-thirty. By that time, the sun is almost about to set. When it becomes dark, she carries the painting stand inside, which is otherwise kept outside, in a corner of the lawn.

Evening tea is with him in the veranda. Sitting on the chair next to the tea table, he thrusts his head into the newspaper, which comes by the afternoon bus. Her place is next to him in the armchair. Same questions. Same answers. But they need to be asked and obviously answered. All the while, she is continuously looking at the distant trees and listens to the rustling leaves.

Gradually it darkens. The sky that was blue becomes pitch black. The shadows of the trees start darkening and merging into the mountains. The hill starts fading away. She sits watching that thin borderline of the trees disappearing into the graying mountains, which in turn is merging with the sky. What remains is only the enormity of a huge black spot.

Leaves are continuously swaying. Branches are shaking convulsively. She can't see them but can hear the rustling of the leaves. When everything disappears, she closes her eyes. But the rustling is still audible.

When he raises his head from the newspaper, he can see her closed eyes. The question of rustling leaves still stands between both of them. He folds the newspaper, keeps it on the tea table and stretches his body. She opens her eyes and stares at the mountains. Time goes by. He looks here and there with unease. Her eyes are still on the rustling leaves. He feels like saying something but keeps quiet. This has almost become an everyday routine.

He is the one who gets up first. As he goes inside, he glances at her incomplete painting, kept in a corner of the hall and moves ahead. Earlier he used to observe it minutely. He could tell which colours have been added or when there hasn't been a change, not even of a single line. But, try as he may, he could never tell what the painting was all about. She never attempts to explain. She expects him to understand. It's wishful thinking to expect outsiders to understand her paintings. Once his colleagues had visited their place and saw the paintings. He didn't know why, but his boss while leaving hinted to her: 'I think you will be able to draw nature very well.' She didn't say anything but he saw she felt dejected. He didn't comment on it and she didn't expect it either.

Although he didn't understand her drawings, one thing was certain. He noticed that the once neat, clear and simple images were gradually becoming more complicated. Bright and lively rainbow colours were overtaken by different shades of dark grey and blue. At times he thought he could see a darkened mountain but did not ask her. In the beginning, he had tried to talk about her drawings and paintings and even encouraged her. Her reaction was never encouraging. Ultimately, he came to the conclusion that it is best to keep mum.

If she exhausted her colours, she would give him the name and number and he would get them while on the way back from office.

These days a canvas stood outside but he noticed that it hardly had any new layers of colours.

THERE WERE TWO MORE engineers staying in the area. Once or twice in a fortnight, they along with their wives would meet. Right from the beginning she had maintained a distance. One of the ladies had once asked her, 'What about children? Is it just the two of you?' From then on, she lost her mood. This question had followed her wherever she went. Earlier she thought only family members and relatives would ask such questions but even strangers started doing the same.

She left her native place and came to reside in the lap of innocent nature but here too the question was hounding her! Strictly speaking, she had long back decided to drop this issue. It wasn't an important one. One has to accept the reality. Why insist on progeny? What difference is it going to make if one doesn't have a child? She had made up her mind that concepts such as 'motherhood leads to fulfilment' are all nonsensical. She didn't have any grudge or a feeling of covetousness towards anyone and if anyone commented on such matters, it's okay. Some would speak out of compassion and others just for the heck of it or out of spite. In fact, she silently laughed inside when someone got uneasy about her frigidity.

But he was very sensitive. And this characteristic of his would seriously annoy her. She used to always feel that one shouldn't be so sensitive. He too didn't have any kind of regret or sorrow for not having a child, but the worry – about how she must be coping with this matter – gnawed him all the time. While raising her spirits, he himself would narrowly slip and collapse.

'At present we don't want a child. We will decide what to do when we are ready. We can even go in for adoption if need be. I'll surely let you know,' was her standard reply, always delivered with the cold dexterity of an adept surgeon.

Despite being so clear to others, her uneasiness went on increasing. Without any reason, her heart started turning inwards. With the need to involve her mind in something, she turned towards colours or sat in the armchair and looked at infinite nature. He made numerous efforts to bring her out of it but the outcome was always the opposite.

'Why are you after me? Not allowing me to sit quietly for even two minutes,' she would say.

'But then what do you do the whole day?'

'Nothing.'

For days together, she would be in a state of sullenness, with literal exchange of only some four to five words and after a while, even his enthusiasm started disappearing.

'Listen. I am a mere engineer, who knows only how to break stones. I don't understand these colours. It will be better if you tell me something,' he asked looking at her canvas.

'Why is the insistence on knowing everything? Certain things are self-explanatory. They need to be understood.' This chapter was also closed.

THERE WAS AN OPEN SPACE round the bungalow. He had employed two people and got it cleaned. He planted flowering shrubs around and creepers at the gate. At the centre was a beautiful green lawn. The hibiscus grew rapidly. He felt that she would take interest in gardening. Perhaps the colourful flowers would make her feel cheerful and then she would get engrossed in it. But hers was a different story. Her sight was fixed on the trees that were far away. She didn't even bother to take heed of the jasmine flowers that were planted at the doorstep.

Only once she had commented on his gardening. Someone had planted 'Raatraani' in the district's government rest-house. The 'Night Queen' was a night-blooming jasmine. It was rare in that area. He remembered seeing one in her courtyard. Thinking she will appreciate his effort, he had brought one of its branches home to be planted.

In the morning when he was about to leave for the mine, seeing that branch of Raatraani resting against the veranda wall, she asked, 'What's this?'

'Yesterday while coming back I saw this Raatraani in the backyard of the guesthouse. It was in full bloom. I asked the gardener to give me a branch.'

'Don't plant it,' she said and went inside. He too left for his work. He had thought of planting it that evening after work but when he came back, he saw that it was already planted. Perhaps the gardener saw it and planted it. Even she must not have noticed it. Else she would have stopped him from doing so. He had always pampered her like a child and, without any questions, he fulfilled her wishes. He had never ever given any preference to his own likes and dislikes but she never understood it. She lost her temper on trivial matters. And these days her mood swings had increased. Creative people are usually moody characters, in their own state of trance. He had some sort of reverence for her and always ignored it. But matters were crossing all limits.

'If you don't like Raatraani then tell me so. I do not insist on planting it but why shouldn't I plant it if I wanted to?' he had asked before leaving for work. Anyway, the gardener had already planted it. And it went on proliferating in full swing by bursting into lush green leaves. She had said what she had to say on the matter. And she thought he had ignored it.

The place from where she could view and hear the far-off lush green trees was now slowly getting blocked by the Raatraani. Now a new tension had come to reside between them. She changed her spot. Instead of sitting in the veranda, she now started sitting inside, placing her chair near the window. From there she could see her beloved dense forest and of course hear its rustling leaves.

In the evening, after his arrival, she would go into a trance.

His paper would be outside on the tea table. She would serve him the tea and come back inside to sit. However, the Raatraani, which was now out of her sight, did not leave her. On the contrary, it pursued her. The flowers that bloom at night would fill their house with their scent. It wasn't that she disliked the fragrance. It was just that her attention, which otherwise used to be fixed on the far-off trees, now started getting distracted. The invisible Raatraani started rankling. Another grudge got tightened.

There was a Raatraani plant at her home. She did not like it much. She didn't even remember it much. For years now, she has stayed away from her home. She had forgotten her house, her family, her village...As it is, there wasn't much to be remembered. The little that she remembers is nothing pleasing – the remains of incompleteness, insecurity, clawing, trauma, bitterness. It's better not to remember. Even the Raatraani wasn't as much a reminder of her house as an irritating distraction. In spite of saying 'No', it was planted.

One day, the maid, who otherwise would enter through the gate without lifting her head, saw something and stood there absolutely still, staring at the Raatraani with a startled look. Walking some fifteen steps in a flurry, she entered the door with fear written all over her face. She went out again and looked very intently at the Raatraani, which had spread close to the wall, but from a distance.

When the maid came back inside, she asked her what had she seen. Her face was as usual very glassy and her eyes were lowered. She did not say a word.

'I had told him not to plant the Raatraani…,' she muttered to herself as she went out. It seemed as if the string of a petticoat was dangling from the branches of the Raatraani. When she saw it, she was almost shaken out of stupor and kept staring at it. Without the maid telling her, she understood what she must have seen. When she was young, her mom used to always say, 'My dear children, don't go too near the Raatraani.' After pestering her mother several times to tell the reason why, her mom revealed her experience. Her mother had avoided telling it because she did not want her children to have any fear in their minds. Somehow she never understood what was so fearful in that matter.

As usual, she took all her art material and set up a new canvas on the lawn. Soon she was completely engrossed in her painting. All the while, she could hear the rustling of those far-off leaves with increasing intensity.

For her, the nearby Raatraani was not in existence at all. Same was the case with the other plants of the garden. She did not see the colours of the leaves and flowers that he had planted and was instead drawn to the distant dark bluish grey shades. Those swaying trees – she felt compelled to draw the leaves with a depth that did not just show movement but also echoed the rustling. If a painting wasn't up to the mark, she discarded it and started another.

One afternoon, a few days later, he came home early. She was so engrossed in her painting that she didn't even realize it until he came and stood close to her.

'Come inside,' he said. 'Don't paint outside.'

She followed him and asked, 'Why?'

'There is a snake in the greenery near the Raatraani. The gardener has seen it in the morning.'

'What's the big deal? Our maid has also seen it. And I see it every day.'

'What?'

'Yes. It comes out in the afternoon to bask in the sun.'

'What are you saying?'

'I had told you right in the beginning not to plant the Raatraani. You didn't listen. After the blooming of the Raatraani, do you expect to find a mongoose instead of snakes? Do you want to know how it looks? If I see it tomorrow, I will draw its picture. Even if I don't see it, I will be able to draw it since I have seen it umpteen times.'

'Aren't you afraid?'

'What's there to be afraid of?'

'Never mind. I will bring all your art material inside.'

He forcibly took her inside.

The next morning, the gardener whacked off the Raatraani and cleared the entire area. She again started having her evening tea with him outside.

Although the Raatraani was uprooted, he was still uneasy. While having tea, at least once he would glance around near the steps.

Looking at the distant trees, which were cajoling with the wind, the rustling sound was obsessively audible to her. Along with it, the fragrance of Raatraani also wafted in.

Days passed after the Raatraani was removed. No one saw

the snake again. Neither he nor she spoke about it. The only thing that was different was her paintings. Whenever he stole a glance at them now, he started noticing scaly turns of coils at the foot of the trees that would be grappling the sky. Sky, trees, leaves, mountains, scales – all had the same greyish-blue colour but with slight variations in shades.

He finished reading the newspaper. He was thinking whether he should get up or not when out of the blue, she remarked, 'How pleasant is the fragrance of Raatraani!'

He was startled – it was horrifying and spine chilling. He felt as if the snake creepily passed by, extremely close to his feet. Initially she was able to hear the rustling of the trees that were almost ten miles away. Now there isn't a single Raatraani plant for miles and miles…

She opened her eyes and, giving a jerk to her neck, looked at him and smiled. She was very sure that he wasn't getting the smell of Raatraani. She just didn't understand one thing. The same fear that she had seen in the eyes of the maid was now reflected in his eyes too. 'What's there to feel so disturbed about the smell of Raatraani?' She didn't understand.

He was dumbstruck and sat looking at her. She coolly got up and went inside. The moment she saw the picture kept in the corner of the hall, she tried to control her smile. Using different shades, she was now able to draw a picture of moving trees. 'But why am I not able to hear the rustling leaves?' The snake entered inside along the edges creepily. She kept staring at it. It mounted atop the stand and slowly entered into a hole near a tree's trunk and disappeared into it.

When he came inside, she must inform him about the snake entering the hole. She stood next to her painting. She could hear the distant rustling and sense the drifting fragrance of Raatraani.

Molestation

THE TICKING OF THE WALL clock indicates that time is passing. Else there is no way of knowing the time, or knowing whether it's day or night. The room is completely blocked from all the four sides. Not a ray of sunlight enters the air-conditioned room. Every morning, the peon sprays some air freshener but by evening it starts smelling musty again. Others either do not notice this or they ignore it as a trivial matter.

'Why do you think so much? We are sitting in an air-conditioned room. That means to some extent the same air is obviously going to circulate inside. On top of that, we are in an old building and our office does not open to the outside. It's okay! Do your work and flee.' Saying so, DK's boss had once dismissed him. He had even tried to broach the topic many times with his colleagues but no one paid any attention.

'Listen, you don't have any work to do. That's why you have the time to get upset over such smells. This is all psychological. DK, better get busy with something…' Ranganathan had once brusquely commented while picking up his bag to go home at the end of the day. From then on, DK stopped talking to anyone on this topic.

Since ten minutes were left for the office to get over, he had to wait. Everyone, from the General Manager to the peon, has to punch a card on entering and leaving office. All the details – who has come, who has gone and when – are automatically registered. All the marketing staff also have to punch their cards. There is no longer any need to sign the muster book like earlier. It's not that anyone will ask any questions if he punched his card ten minutes before time. But then why unnecessarily put himself in a position where he may have to give reasons? Initially everyone had opposed the punching system, but all protests gradually subsided. Those who had opposed left one by one – some on their own, some resigned, some were sacked and some were given a golden handshake and kicked out. Now who is left to oppose? When the boss himself punches the card, who will oppose?

He picked up the phone.

Whom to dial? Kept it back again.

Once Shankar had commented, 'Feels so good to take

home the salary without doing any work.' Shankar too does not have any work. He sits on a revolving chair next to the receptionist, adjacent to the medical room. In this new office, with all the new décor, he doesn't know where his old wooden stool has disappeared.

I should call Sudhakar.

He again lifted the phone, but couldn't get through.

It's always convenient when he goes with Sudhakar, because they can go together from CST, get down at Ghatkopar, at times go to the bar at the corner of the road, sit for a while and then leave for home. At least some time is killed. But, his head was aching very badly that day.

'I know there is very little work and it gets very boring but I must hold on to this job at any cost. Where will I get another job? Even if I get one, it won't be as good as this – plus less salary with new tensions. The management has also changed – new people, new policies – then why to expect the same old system. Till now no one has touched me. Good post, fat salary, come on time, go on time. In a new place, who knows what work may come my way and what sort of responsibility will be thrust on me? Let me go on with it instead of thinking about the future.'

DK lifted his bag, kept it on the table, opened it, took out his water bottle and gulped some water. While drinking, he took care not to spill any. Closing the lid tightly, he wrapped the bottle again in a plastic bag, kept it back in his bag and wiped the drops of water on his lips with his wrist. He felt a bit better.

He tried to call up Sudhakar again. No one picked up.

He must have already left. Or perhaps he was getting ready to leave.

Just then his phone rang.

'Yes?'

'DK?'

'Speaking.'

'Come and meet me before leaving.'

'Yes sir.'

He felt relieved. Boss has called him after so many days. But why was he called? He was suddenly petrified. Usually the boss is in the habit of handing over all important matters at the end of the day. It must be something important. 'I don't even have any urgent assignment right now in hand. Why did he call me?'

He realized that he was perspiring a bit. His palms had become wet. DK rubbed them against each other and tried to dry them. 'Before leaving' means after five.

His uneasiness grew. He again opened his bag, drank water without spilling a drop and kept the bottle back. Calling up Sudhakar again, he got through this time. However, now there was no question of meeting him as he did not know how much time the boss was going to take.

'Yes DK?'

'What's up?'

'Nothing. Getting ready to leave for the day. I hope we are meeting at VT!'

Sudhakar is aware that DK calls him only if they are to

36

meet up.

'No, not today.'

'Why? Got busy?'

'No. Boss has asked me to meet him before leaving.'

'So what's the big deal? It will get over in five-ten minutes. I'll wait. No problem. After you are done, call me up. That's all. Both of us will leave together.'

DK was quite uneasy. He wasn't sure how long it would take. Then again he would have to call up Sudhakar and inform him if he got delayed.

'No. Let's not meet today. I don't know what the nature of work is and if it goes on for a long time, I won't be able to come out and inform you. It's better you don't wait. What you can do is leave some five-ten minutes late. If I'm done, I'll call you up. Else you go ahead and leave.'

'Okay. I feel we will be able to meet. As it is, even I have to wait for a while. Let's see.'

DK kept the phone down and looked at his watch.

He had never before felt such apprehension while going to meet the boss. He had also worked under many. But these days he quivered.

At other times DK never asked 'May I come in, sir?' but that day while opening the door, he did.

Without looking up, the boss said, 'Yes.'

DK stood with his hands clutching the back of the visitor's chair.

'Please sit. Just wait for two minutes.'

DK sat down slowly. Since he had said 'please sit', that

means it is something important. Else, when does he have the time to spare?

Again, even in the air-conditioned room, he felt as if he was perspiring.

Boss looked up and said, 'I am going to give you an assignment. Handle it carefully. It shouldn't be messed up. I really don't understand – why do people unnecessarily fall into trouble?' Saying so, he opened the drawer of his desk and took out some files. Removing a thin one, he kept back all the others inside. 'Take a look at this. Our medical representative (MR) from Aurangabad has messed up. I don't know exactly what he has done but it seems a police complaint has been lodged against him. The case may reach the court also.'

'What has he done?'

'Someone has lodged a complaint against him in the police station. On the eve of New Year's day, he drank and romped around. The news was printed in the local newspaper. The company's name has unnecessarily got dragged into it. One of our directors was there on a sightseeing trip to Ajanta-Ellora caves, along with his family. Someone informed him. He then informed the admin. The chairman is very upset and had screamed, "Fire the bastard". But we cannot take any hasty steps.'

DK was thinking, 'Why is he telling me all these details? What have I got to do with it?' But asking him won't be right. So he quietly listened. While talking, the boss picked up a glass of water, drank it and browsed through the file. 'The MD had sent the matter to our legal advisor. According to the legal advisor, we cannot take immediate action against that rascal. He has suggested a departmental enquiry.

'If we appoint a lawyer for the enquiry, we will have to shell out money like water. Also, if that lawyer while doing his enquiry bombards questions on our marketing system, then unnecessarily official matters will come under a scanner. And then there won't be any control of ours on this enquiry. Plus a copy of the report needs to be submitted to the Labour Welfare Association's officer. Badlapurkar is a very shrewd person. Once he realizes that he is going to be trapped, he won't hesitate to hit back at the company. So the case has to be handled very diplomatically.'

'Who is this Badlapurkar?'

'Same one, our MR from Aurangabad.'

'You mean that strapping brawny fellow?'

'Yes. The same one. So I feel you only should take up this matter.'

'But sir, I don't have any legal background.'

'That's okay. At least we can show the government and the court that we have taken some action. That is the first thing and second, we must know about his movements. So it's necessary for you to go and get information on him.'

'Yes, sir,' said DK.

After so many days, the boss has assigned him some important work. He felt he had no reason to resist doing the job.

'Don't worry, sir. I will go through the case and report to you tomorrow. I have earlier handled the Aurangabad

Division. So I have few acquaintances there. I don't think we will face any problem.'

'That's right.' Boss gave him the file.

From his experience, he knew that whenever sir says, 'That's right,' it means 'enough…now move out'.

He took the file and went back to his cabin. He was almost half an hour with the boss. Sudhakar must have definitely left. He once again opened his bag, took out the water bottle and drank the remaining water. He browsed through the file. Why unnecessarily take work home? If he takes his office work home, then what work will he have in office?

Reaching home that night, he called up his friend Sawant. After talking over few other matters, he told him the reason why he had called him up.

'The case is easy to handle. Write down all the details. Give a draft to me to read. I will guide you on how to conduct an enquiry. It is not that difficult. But the important part is: before you come to any conclusion, you need to give a chance to the concerned person to state his or her side of the story. That way, you won't be blamed for taking a one-sided decision.'

'Okay, then, when shall we meet?'

'Call me up next week on Monday. We will meet in the afternoon or after five.'

The next day, DK read each and every word in the file. Except the news item from the daily Devgiri, there was no other information in it. He jotted down certain points:

– Visit Aurangabad

– Seek information from the police about the case

– Meet Badlapurkar

He called up the boss over the intercom. 'After five' was the answer. Till then, how to while away the time? He called up Sudhakar.

'I waited for you for a long time yesterday. But then finally left.'

'Yes. My meeting went on for quite some time.'

'Shall we meet today? But I will be a bit late. Might be six-thirty.'

'Yes, it's okay. Even I am going to be late.'

Exactly at five past five, DK knocked at the boss's door. Without asking 'May I come in?' he entered and gave him an update.

'That means you need to go to Aurangabad. Right? Send the proposal and start off. Don't waste time.' He didn't have much time, so without wasting time in discussion, he cut short the topic.

'Yes sir.'

DK happily came out. He was to go on tour for office work. He immediately sent a notice to General Manager, Administration.

Getting down at Ghatkopar with Sudhakar, DK said, 'It's just eight-thirty. Let's sit for some time.' Saying so, they entered the bar.

'What does your boss want?' Sudhakar directly came to the point. DK always discussed freely with him about office matters such as the changing office environment and his perpetual fear of losing the job. Sudhakar was aware of everything and even he realized that some important development must have taken place.

'You know, the boss has asked me to handle a case. One of our MRs has got stuck in a serious matter. He and his wife had gone for some New Year's party along with a friend. From there they went to that friend's house. There was a fight and the friend has lodged a complaint against him.'

'Where?'

'With the police. It has become a big issue in the local newspapers. It seems the MR was called by the police. They have taken his statement, but let him go. Don't know whether they are going to file a case against him. The matter has reached the ears of the company's director. I have been asked to conduct a departmental enquiry. What a nonsensical problem! I don't even know what labour law is. I may go to do one thing and it may end up as something else. I will soon go to Aurangabad and finish it off once and for all.'

'Cheers!' they toasted and began to drink the beer.

Sudhakar took the first sip. 'Have you gone mad or crazy? Why are you finishing it off so early? Since your director has brought the issue to the notice of the administration, it is already a top priority work and no one will say anything even if it is prolonged. Chill. Work at a leisurely pace. You don't have any other work than killing time at office. Why this hurry? Else you will be considered as a 'surplus' and sacked from the job. And tell me something, who is going to employ you at this age?' Sudhakar broke into a thunderous artificial laugh. DK also joined in.

Sudhakar had a point.

'Do one thing. Go to Aurangabad on Monday. Collect all the information. Don't decide upon anything. Then meet that friend of yours who is an advocate and take his advice. Ask him the methodology of conducting an enquiry. And an important thing – tell him that this enquiry should not get over quickly; it should be prolonged. Accordingly, he will give you the advice. Else there is no guarantee. You may finish it off within two days and return!'

It had rained lightly just before DK got down at the Aurangabad airport. As it was an untimely shower, there was a sudden increase in the humidity and temperature.

The airport was not very crowded. He was not carrying much luggage – just a day's clothes and that thin file. Taking the bag in his hand, he went straight outside. There was a person from the hotel standing with a placard with his name on it. He hadn't informed anyone in the office.

Hotel Prize was in the main city but in the Civil Lines area. There were big roads with trees on both sides and no noise of traffic. When he pushed aside the curtain in his room, he could see the Bibi Ka Maqbara. Earlier, there were hardly any hotels good enough to stay in. Now one could see four-star hotels all over the city.

The first thing he had to do was to go to the police station and collect information. After that, he had to contact the office, talk with the concerned MR, meet the party who had lodged the complaint and leave. He placed an order for tea and asked the operator to connect him to his residential number. He informed his wife that he had reached safe and sound, enquired if there was any call for him and disconnected the line.

Before leaving home, he had spoken with the MLA sahib, who had in turn called up the police station in Aurangabad, informed them that his friend would be visiting, and asked them to provide the necessary help. The MLA also gave DK the name of the concerned police inspector. 'I could have accompanied you but I need to go urgently to Delhi. If you have any problem, you can call up my son. His name is Rajwardhan.'

On reaching Aurangabad, DK took out his diary and dialed up a number. It rang for a long time.

'Kabutarkhana Police Station!'

'Can I speak to Jamkar Sir?'

'No. He hasn't come as yet. May I know who this is?'

'I am DK, regional manager of Semtel.'

'Oh yes sir. May I help you?'

'Tell Jamkar Sir that I called. I am at Hotel Prize, Room No. 114. When is he expected?'

'No idea, sir. But he usually comes by eleven, eleven-thirty. Should I give any other message?'

'No. Ask him to call me up.'

'Sure sir.'

He took out the blue file to go through the photocopy of the news article. The name of the person who had lodged the complaint was mentioned as Dhanraj Nahar. It was also mentioned that he owned a hardware shop somewhere opposite the High Court. DK jotted down the name. He didn't find a directory in the room and asked the receptionist to send one. There were some ten-twelve Nahars. From among those, he found Dhanraj and dialed his number.

'Hello!'

'Is it Dhanraj Nahar?'

'Yes speaking.'

'Namaskar! I am DK here, regional manager from Semtel.'

Silence. After some time – 'Yes. What do you want?'

'I don't have any personal work with you, but I have come down from Mumbai to do the enquiry on the case filed by you against an MR from our company.'

There was no response.

'We are expecting some cooperation from your side. Can I come to meet you?'

'No. There is no need to. We have already lodged a complaint with the police. What else needs to be discussed? The case is going to come up in court.'

'Mr Nahar, first of all, on behalf of the company, I beg your forgiveness. Our chairman himself has appointed me for the departmental enquiry. Even we are of the stand that if our person has done anything wrong, he must be punished.'

'Let it be. You do whatever you want but don't involve me in your official matters.'

'Yes. You are right. But if you cooperate, we will be able to take proper legal action.'

'What cooperation do you want? First fire that bastard. He and his wife must die of hunger.'

DK realized there was no point in talking to him any further. But before returning, it was very important for him to get the complete information. The news article didn't carry much and he was unable to figure out what exactly Badlapurkar had done. 'Caused a sensation, lodged a complaint in the police station' – such broad statements did not reveal anything.

Removing his shirt, he lay down on the bed. He removed his wrist-watch that was pricking him and placed it on the side table. He then stretched himself regally and went off to sleep. He must have hardly slept for ten minutes when the phone rang. He heard it ringing as if in a dream. It was difficult for him to come out of languor. Initially, he couldn't recollect where he was. Then he realized with a start that the phone was ringing.

'Namaskar! I am Inspector Jamkar here.'

'Namaskar! I have come down to Aurangabad in connection with our MR's case.'

'Oh yes. MLA sahib has asked me to provide you with whatever help you require. What is your programme today?'

'Nothing special. You tell me when I can meet you.'

'Right now it's quarter to twelve. I will require another hour or two to complete my work. After that I can come over. I won't be able to take the papers out, but I will go through the file and give you all the details.'

'Yes, that will do. I want to know the details of the case, its nature, what can be done and what it may lead to.'

'I will be there by two-thirty. I hope I won't be disturbing you!'

'No, not at all.'

Keeping the phone down, DK lay down on the bed again. Bibi Ka Maqbara was visible from the window. Its dome was shining in the bright sunlight. Now there was no chance of feeling sleepy. If he got the information of the case, it meant that half his work was done. He was happy with the progress he was making.

He felt too lazy to get up and go down to the restaurant for lunch. He browsed through Lokmat, a local newspaper. It carried big photographs of a rally for drinking water. Putting the newspaper aside, he dialed room service and placed his order for lunch, 'One stuffed brinjal, rice, two chapattis, dal fry and mineral water.'

By the time he finished his lunch, it was one-thirty. He didn't have any acquaintances in Aurangabad. So whose place to visit? He knew some businessmen but all must be busy in their own work. With the cool air of the AC and the TV on, he remained lying on his bed.

Exactly at two-thirty, Inspector Jamkar called up from the reception. DK asked him to come upstairs to his room. Both shook hands. The inspector sat on the sofa and DK on a chair.

'What would you like to have – tea, coffee or something cold?'

'A cold drink will be fine.'

DK called up at the reception. 'Please send two Thumbs

Up to Room No. 114.'

'I suppose you must be slightly aware of the case. It's a case of molestation. The lady herself has lodged it. Even her husband was along with her. To top it, initially Badlapurkar's wife had also agreed to and supported what Dhanraj's wife said. So the case has become a bit serious. Later she produced an affidavit and changed her statement. Now nothing is in our hands. Actually speaking, all of them are educated people, but it's surprising the way they behaved! Unnecessarily, even your company's name is getting maligned.'

'I have brought the copy of the FIR but couldn't get copies of the other statements. At least you will get an idea of what has taken place from this report.'

He handed a vertically folded photocopy of the FIR to DK. Browsing through it, DK kept it aside. Reading that paper seemed to be an ordeal.

'We are done with the statements. Now we need to frame charges. Once that is done, the case will be ready to stand in the court. When it reaches the court, the prosecution part will be done by the court. But such cases don't endure for long. To top it, both the couples were drunk.'

'You mean even Mrs Badlapurkar!'

'Yes, that night even she came with the Nahars to lodge a complaint against her own husband. If she hadn't done so, we wouldn't have taken much heed. As it is, on every New Year's eve there is always some row or the other, quarrel or dispute that takes place and this has become a nuisance for us. . .

'These two couples had been to a New Year's party, drank

a lot of beer, and there Badlapurkar had a heated argument with the waiter. After that, all four of them went home in Dhanraj's car. There also they must have boozed. Wives might not have drunk but we don't know. That was the time when this molestation supposedly took place.'

DK kept listening.

'If both parties compromise, it will be good for us. We will be saved from further vexation. Once the case starts, can't predict for how many days, months or years it will continue. I hope you remember Gill's case, which went on for years together! Moreover, you are supposed to remain present on whichever date has been allotted to you. An unnecessary waste of time! But if you try to pressurize from the company's side, may be matters will speed up.'

'Yes, I understand. But we are in no way acquainted with that Dhanraj, nor is he our distributor. Why will he listen to us?'

'No. I mean, why will he be enthusiastic about the case? Tomorrow when it starts and his wife will be made to stand in the witness box, he will realize his folly. The way lawyers will throw questions on her won't be funny. If influential people like you request and make him see reason, I don't think he will refuse. In fact, I feel he will even try his best to get out of it.

'They were in a drunken state and irked. Without thinking of the consequences, they came to the police station and lodged a complaint. That foolish Mrs Badlapurkar left her husband lying on Dhanraj's sofa and came along with both of them to the police station. From there all three went back. This lady put her husband into a rickshaw at 3 a.m. and took him home. Now tell me – isn't all this ridiculous and troublesome for people like us?'

Jamkar went on talking and DK went on looking at the paper in his hand. He has got the necessary information. Jamkar started drifting away from the main topic. Even if he paid attention, it would be difficult to trace which string the Inspector was harping on.

Meanwhile the waiter came. He opened the bottle of Thumbs Up and poured the drink. DK kept on staring at the turbid foam effervescing from the dark auburn-coloured cold drink.

Saying 'Please have', he started drinking. On hindsight, he should have offered beer to the inspector. But perhaps it was for the best; he would have wasted more time in that. He noted down the clauses that could be levelled while confirming the allegations. By then, both of them finished their drinks. DK wrote down Jamkar's residential phone numbers in his diary. He asked him to let him know if he got any other information or if any further developments took place. Saying so, he gave his own residence number.

After Jamkar left, DK opened his spiral notebook. This was a very old habit that he had developed when he was working for Lipton Tea Company. His boss, a Parsi, had the habit of immediately making note of any important details in a small notebook. He had also strictly instructed all his subordinates to do the same and after meetings, he would collect all the notebooks to check. DK's habit stayed with him and he benefited a lot from the same.

He noted down the information that he got from the inspector. It took ten minutes but he wrote everything. His notebook was systematic and the details were in the manner of an official report: Date–31st December, 1998; time–midnight, name, age, permanent address, telephone number, husband's name, occupation – service, service address, phone number, address of the accused. He included the IPC section and the points made by Jamkar.

The FIR did not carry more information than what Jamkar had provided. He folded that paper and kept it in the notebook. Remembering that he had forgotten a vital point, he again opened the book – Semtel's manager of Aurangabad office had met Jamkar and requested to take back the complaint at any cost.

He looked at the watch. It was four-thirty. He picked up the phone.

'Semtel.'

'Can I speak to Mr Inamdar?'

'Speaking.'

'I am DK here.'

'Yes sir.'

'I am in Aurangabad. What is your programme?'

'Nothing special, sir. But when did you arrive? If you had informed me, I would have come to receive you. In which hotel have you booked your stay?'

'In Hotel Prize. Don't go anywhere. I am coming. Might

be late – will give you a tinkle.'

'Yes sir.'

Inamdar kept the phone down but was bemused. Why had DK come here? There must be some special reason. For ten years he had been handling the Aurangabad office. If anyone comes from the head office, he looks after their arrangements. He had never given a chance to anyone to point out any fault in this work. But, at the same time, he had taken utmost care not to allow any person who has come from Mumbai to meet any of the members from his office privately.

By six-thirty in the evening, almost the entire staff had finished their work and left. He asked only his peon to wait.

When DK arrived, he ushered him into his cabin while yelling at his peon, 'Two special teas.' Then he turned to DK and asked, 'Would you like to have a sandwich, dosa or anything else?'

'No, only tea.'

DK sat down. The table was looking clean. But outside there were heap of files with dust everywhere.

'By the way, how's Mumbai?'

'Good. Everything's fine.'

'I heard everything has become computerized.'

'Yes, paperless offices. Soon other regional offices are also going to be updated. You are lucky that you have a peon. We don't have a peon in the Mumbai office. We bring our own tea or coffee in a paper cup from a machine that has been installed. There is no need to carry files from here to there. Everything is computerized.'

'Oh wow!' Inamdar enthused like a schoolboy. They chatted about various topics. As the tea came, DK broached the topic he had come for.

'What is the Badlapurkar matter?'

Inamdar kept back the cup he had lifted. He didn't expect such a question from DK. Especially because he was under the impression that no one knew about the matter.

'It's a police matter. A complaint has been lodged against him to the police. But it will be settled. Don't worry. It's not that serious.'

'What is the actual matter? Do you know that it has reached up to the chairman? He has taken a serious note. You should have informed the head office earlier.'

'Yes, I know, but the matter isn't that serious. And the poor fellow – he cried and wants to cover it up and settle mutually. Why to spoil anyone's record? That's the reason I didn't reveal it to anyone.'

'What had exactly happened? Tell me.'

'Actually even I don't know. He had been to some New Year's party. Boozed a lot and created a scene along with his friends. They have lodged a complaint against him.'

DK could see that Inamdar knew everything but wasn't letting out anything.

'Does everyone know in the office?'

'Yes. Everyone knows. But it is his personal matter. It has nothing to do with the company.' Inamdar tried to justify.

'Listen Inamdar, the management has decided to take action. I have been given the charge of the case.'

'Oh! Yes sir. Then tell me. What can I do?'

'Departmental enquiry needs to be conducted but there is still some time for it. Initially, a primary report has to be prepared and given to the top management. You do one thing – give me in writing all the information you have. I am going back by the evening flight tomorrow. Submit it before that, and where is that Badlapurkar?'

'He is here only. I mean, he had come in the morning. Should I call him?'

'No. I will come tomorrow in the afternoon. See to it that he doesn't go anywhere. It won't look good to talk in front of everyone. Let me use your cabin.'

'Okay, sir.'

They talked about other topics. Despite his protests, Inamdar took DK out for dinner and then dropped him back at the hotel. He asked about the next day – 'What time are you coming? Should I come to pick you up?' and then left.

In the morning at 8 o'clock, Inamdar called him up.

'Sir, have you read today's paper?'

DK had the paper in his hand. 'Anything special?'

'The local newspaper is carrying the news regarding that case. It says that Semtel's senior official, DK Rangachari, has arrived in Aurangabad for an enquiry.'

DK's brows knit.

'But who has informed them?'

'No idea, sir. In fact I was with you till ten-thirty. Should I get the paper?'

54

'No, it's okay.'

He did not have to search for it. On the front page, at the left hand bottom corner, there was a two-paragraph news item. Semtel's senior official DK Rangachari in Aurangabad for enquiry – the nature of the complaint against Badlapurkar was also mentioned.

Unable to understand how the news got leaked, he read it again and again. He then kept that paper in the file. By nine-thirty, he was ready. His thoughts were interrupted by the ringing phone. Wondering who it was, he picked up the phone.

'Can I speak to DK sir?'

'Speaking.'

'Sir, I am Badlapurkar here. Sorry sir, I must have disturbed you. I am at the reception. Wanted to meet you, sir.'

How come he has come here? 'Well, I was going to meet in the office. So let's see you there only,' he told him.

'I will be there in the office but if you give me a chance to meet you now, I will be highly obliged. I won't take much of your time.'

'Very well. Come on up.' Anyway, he wasn't doing anything.

Badlapurkar knocked on the door and came in. His wife followed him. They sat down awkwardly and were clearly nervous. DK observed them carefully.

'Sir, I read in the newspaper that you have come down for the enquiry. In the office, only I will be able to meet you. But my wife said that even she would like to meet you and beg your pardon. So I have brought her here.'

'You weren't in your wits till the case went to the police station. I mean…I don't have to say anything regarding that, but when the matters reach the court, unnecessarily the company's name gets spoiled. So an enquiry is a must.'

'I am ready to give any kind of cooperation required for the enquiry. Actually nothing inappropriate took place. Matters have been blown out of proportion. My friend Dhanraj was quite angry so without any reason he has complained to the police. If you want, you can ask my wife. She was also present there. Now you only tell me, in front of my wife and friend how can I molest anybody!'

Cutting him in the middle, DK asked, 'What will you have – tea or coffee?'

'Nothing sir.'

Ignoring him, DK asked, 'Tea?'

Mrs Badlapurkar was quiet but listening intently.

DK rang the bell two-three times. No one came.

Badlapurkar got up. 'Sir, I will order tea,' he said and went out. His wife looked around the room.

'You were present there. Right? What had happened exactly?'

'Should I tell you the truth, sir? I don't remember anything. But whatever that Mrs Dhanraj is saying is not true at all. In fact we had an argument between us and getting annoyed over it, Dhanraj went to the police station.'

'But it seems they have your statement too.'

'Yes. I had spoken one thing and they had written down something else. I told them that but they were not ready to listen. So our lawyer drafted an affidavit and I submitted it to them.'

Badlapurkar came back.

'Have asked for three teas.'

'Are you aware that because of your statement your husband has got entangled into a very big problem?'

'This is where I had gone wrong. We are ready to do whatever you tell, but please help us out of this situation. We will be extremely grateful to you, sir.' She removed a small handkerchief from her purse and wiped her tears.

'Sir, I am not scared about the case. Because it won't last long. I even feel that there are chances of them withdrawing the case. However, sir, I need some time. Please don't take any departmental action against me. I will be facing a lot of hardships. I have three school-going children. I have an ailing mother staying with me. The responsibility of the entire family is on me, sir. Please sir…'

DK sipped his tea slowly and said, 'I understand but I am sorry. By rule, an enquiry has to be done because the complaint has reached the higher authorities.'

'Sir, please save me at any cost,' said Badlapurkar and fell at his feet.

'Oh no! What are you doing? Basically, you and me, we both are servants of the company. I will try my best. But please see to it that you don't fall into any other trouble.'

Saying 'No sir' together, they left the room.

DK checked out at three from the hotel and went to the office, which looked cleaner. Inamdar came out, felicitated him with a bouquet and welcomed him and took him to his cabin.

After a cup of tea, Inamdar provided him with the branch details.

'Should I send Badlapurkar inside? Take your own time to wind up. Till then, I will have a look outside and check if there is any pending work.'

DK didn't say anything.

Badlapurkar came inside and stood.

'Sit.'

DK's thoughts were racing. What must be his salary, how much incentive must he be getting and he is taking his wife to parties, drinks quite some amount of beer – what does all this mean?

'Listen. I am not going to start any enquiry right now. You will get an official notice for the same. At that time if you want, you can take your lawyer's help. Today I am here to talk to you as one of your senior colleagues. Let me know all the details – what has taken place, how has it taken place, what is the scene with the police and what is going to be your defence.'

'Thank you very much, sir. I will tell you everything,' said the nervous man. He then proceeded to narrate the same story with a small difference. According to him, Mrs Dhanraj had pressurized his wife to write down the statement.

'That means your entire stress is on the fact that your wife had been pressurized to give the statement. Can I call your wife for the enquiry?'

'Yes sir.'

'Ask her.'

'Yes sir. I'll ask her. We have already given an affidavit regarding the same to the police.'

'Okay. Get a copy of it the next time.'

'Sure sir. I'll get it.'

'You will get a letter. Date and time will be informed to you. Come accordingly. But in the meantime, if there are any developments, call me up at Mumbai and let me know.'

'Sure sir. I will let you know.'

Badlapurkar went out and Inamdar came in.

'So, what has our hero got to say?' he asked with a laugh.

'He is completely finished. Matter seems to have got too intricate.'

Inamdar became cautious, 'Is that so?'

But DK didn't say anything further. He could only visualize his AC room, computer, telephone and the hanging empty time.

Inamdar dropped him in his car at the airport. Fortunately the flight was on time. After the seat-belt sign went off, he removed his notebook. After thinking for some time, he wrote down certain points.

– Company headquarters must be immediately informed; Inamdar should be transferred

– Suspend Badlapurkar and complete the enquiry by April

– Badlapurkar's transfer must be done to Nasik (punishment transfer)

The fourth point he did not write.

Make arrangements for the case to go on. Dhanraj should not compromise.

The Parsik Mountain Range near Mumbai started coming into view. DK closed his notebook and kept it inside. He knew he would be frequently getting this view of the Parsik Mountains.

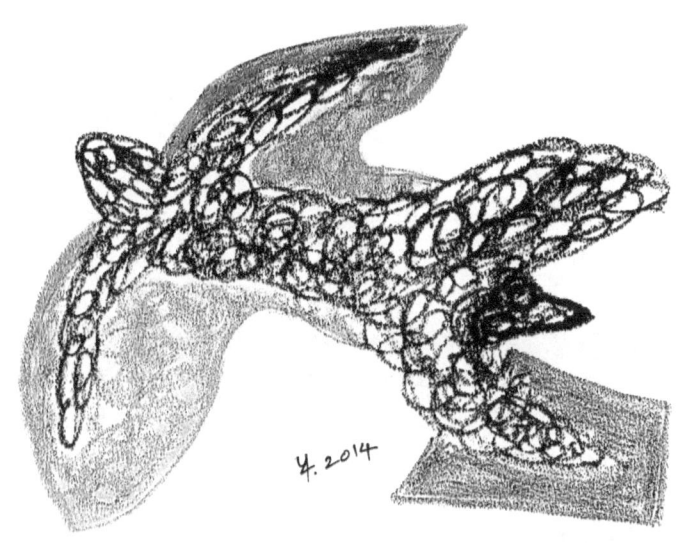

Dissection

THE FROG GOT A LESSER DOSE *of chloroform and I could feel a feeble pulse. Fingers slip over his pale skin. It takes time to wrestle him down with pins hammered through his four legs. The wax platform at the bottom of the dissection pot has thinned down due to overuse and holding the frog still becomes a slippery process. Madam has not yet announced the system that we will be studying today.*

I agree. I do not understand certain things. I am a little slow on the uptake. It doesn't matter how much time someone takes to teach me certain things, I still find them difficult to understand. Not just that. I do not seem to have enough motivation to learn.

Certain things provoke an unreasonable anger. My college. Horrible! Nothing much to speak or write about. Benches are old and loose nails scrape your trousers and your skin every time you squeeze by. Recently, my new trousers got torn by one of those scoundrels. I got irritated and kicked the bench so violently that it splintered, but I hurt my leg.

The first period is at 7 a.m. Normally I miss it. It's followed by a second period, then there is a twenty-minute recess to loiter around, looking at known and unknown faces. Once you enter the canteen, it's difficult to get back to your classes. Four-five cigarettes, some music, some gossip with friends.

Then back to your room, a quick bath if hot water comes out of the geyser. Sometimes I feel like singing while taking a shower and then come out whistling a tune. I squeeze water out of my wet clothes, put them out to dry in the room, comb my wet hair, don't apply hair oil, go to the mess and eat the 'mess' that is served with my eyes closed.

Hmm. I have laid it on its back and removed the skin from its stomach. Exactly as told by madam.

The washbasin is always stinking. I feel like throwing out whatever I have gulped. The sink is full of half-eaten vegetables, grains of rice, coughed-out globs of phlegm…it is nauseating to wash hands. Disgusting! Fucking dirty place! No one ever bothers to clean it despite repeated complaints. There is no mukhwas (mouth fresheners) on the tray. When we ask for it, the manager, Sawant, gives it reluctantly. We call him 'Damager'. He keeps on smiling like a nut. Bony fellow.

Keeps his head buried in one or the other book picked up from the footpath – mostly a detective story. Ever since his wife ran away with one of the boys, he keeps himself busy reading stories.

I am still unfamiliar with the needle. So sharp, it simply pierces. Madam has shown us many times how to hold and insert. But somehow, I am not skilful enough. I am impatient and unsure. It goes deeper than required damaging inner organs. Madam's fingers are very skilled and experienced. She pierces the needle carefully and removes the outer skin without much damage. It's a skill worth observing. After the skin, she pushes aside muscles to bare organs hidden inside. Madam keeps a constant watch on what I am doing. I think she is aware that I cannot handle a needle. So far I have done four dissections of a frog but am still to acquire the basic skill of removing the outer skin. If my needle goes deep inside, madam comes and snatches the needle from my hand.

It is almost 12 noon. After lunch, I feel a little sleepy due to the old movie songs buzzing in the nearby Irani restaurant. Sometimes I don't get to sleep as someone or the other peeps in. Then I just lie down. I feel better after my afternoon siesta. Otherwise, what else to do? Once on the bed, there are no worries! Nothing like a good sound sleep after lunch! I'm known as the Night King. I can remain awake till the wee hours of the morning. As exams approach, all the guys want me to wake them up. Someone wants to wake up at 3 a.m.; another is okay with 4 a.m. or 5:30 a.m. I go to their rooms, yell at them to wake up once or twice. If they respond well and good, or I just go back to my insomnia. I cannot keep banging on their doors to jolt them out of somnolence.

Use a scalpel. Take a cross-section. It's easy and doesn't damage veins; release a lot of blood in the dissection pot. Madam has repeated this dictum several hundred times. And almost everyone including me is now taking cross-sections once the outer skin is removed.

The Irani restaurant adjacent to the college is always open. Day and night. Whenever we get time we keep circling around it. Our table is fixed. It's near a window so one can see a lot people coming and going. He has a good collection of records, old and new, rock and classic. We listen as per our mood and subject other customers to our taste. Normally no one objects to our choice. We keep on sipping endless cups of tea. Beer is not affordable so we take it only occasionally at night. As usual we leave the table by 9.30 p.m. to catch the mess 'Damager' before he closes his shop.

'Which system are we doing today?' I nonchalantly ask Prabhakar. Engrossed in dissection, he says 'nervous' without lifting his head. 'One has to remove the digestive system – right?' 'Right.'

I received a letter from uncle. He keeps on writing occasionally. Study hard, don't neglect your health, your mother's health is not very good, this season crop has almost failed, work on new irrigation dam is still on. He goes on and on. I don't feel like going back to the village. Nor can I concentrate here.

The digestive system has to be removed. Can it be removed permanently? There will be no stomach to feed. It would be great.

64

However, it isn't good to get involved in matters of the stomach. Just make a few incisions and remove it. I stare out of the window; one big dark cloud is floating in the air.

Every morning, Rakhma sweeps the hostel ground. I keep on watching her from the tiny balcony while brushing my teeth. 'Rakhme, Oye Rakhme,' the peon keeps on yelling. She does not reply. Apart from the rasping of her heavy broom, there is no sound. Papers, old bottles, dry crimson leaves of gulmohar, used condoms...she is oblivious to the broom's findings. Uneasy, I watch her. She completes her chore, squats near the gulmohar tree and breastfeeds her growing child.

'Sir, I have some problems.'

'Okay, meet me after the period is over.'

The doubts, however, remain doubts. Who will clarify? Just mug and vomit during examinations and get marks. That's all! What you know or don't know doesn't matter.

'Nagobala doodh...Milk for a cobra' someone shouts from the back benches. The professor thinks they have nicknamed him 'cobra'. 'Who's that idiot?' he screams. Silence. 'You, you, you, get up,' he points a finger at me. I look around and reluctantly get up, hurt and resentful. 'Just get out.' Okay, no hassles! I start walking out of the class. Everybody stares at me. I feel good, as if I have won an award.

Once I walk out of the class, I feel like trudging towards the restaurant. Tea and cigarette. He gives the change back without saying a word or any acknowledgement. Irani Baba looks like a karmayogi – a mystic who does not bother about the fruits of his labour! He puts on the juke box but hardly listens to its outpourings. He has no choice of his own.

'Tina, Tina baby, are you listening to what I am saying? You must get all right and must become hale and hearty. Where is madam?' Such a sweet nice girl madam has but she can't move. Her limbs are numb. She can't walk. She is very weak. She is always in her wheelchair with a teddy in her lap and staring out of the window. When you call out 'Tina', she turns and smiles – a very cute smile, without any trace of pain, embarrassment or words.

The scalpel slips as I am staring out of the window. Alarmed, I bend to pick it up and my eyes meet madam's questioning glance. She is watching me and my clumsiness.

'Haven't you got a dissection box? How many times have I told you to bring it? Everybody should have it. Without it how are you going to learn dissection? This is the fifth class and you still do not have your own box!' One allegation after another. She has tied her hair into a ponytail. What do I tell her? I am not used to being rebuked. Reluctantly, I inform her that I am really economically backward and cannot afford an expensive dissection box. She promptly goes to her cupboard, takes out an old dissection box and hands it over saying that this is yours till you get your own.

I am still using the old one given by her. Once I had gone to her place in connection with organizing a two-day trip. I like Tina, so I now go there once a week without any obvious reason. She hardly talks. When you talk with her, Tina does not say anything but listens attentively to what you have to say to her or what you tell madam. And while talking you look at her, she just smiles and looks out of the window. Madam's mother brings out a tray of tea for both of us. While coming out she gives a sly and suspicious glance. She merely says, 'Hello, how are you?' and disappears into an inner room. Once when madam was not at home, she had reminisced about madam's childhood days and her native village. Madam does not usually like to talk about herself. It depends on her mood. If she is in the mood, she will talk at length, otherwise merely keeps quiet. If she is not communicative, I just say hello to her, talk to Tina and leave. If I do not visit them for a fortnight, she will remind me that Tina has been asking for me.

My encounters with them are an escape from loneliness and homesickness.

I extricate the digestive system without much of a mess. 'Yes madam' I exclaim amidst the dissection, as she takes the roll call. Roll call over. Madam has rearranged her five-yard sari by brushing away wrinkles with fragile fingers. She dusts the roll-call muster and now she will keep it in the top shelf of her cupboard...I do not know what this frog had eaten but his tummy appears dark green and is hard as a stone.

We were bubbly and boisterous during our trip, talking about anything under the sun. Someone saw a creeper crawling up a huge peepal tree and said, 'Oh, what a beautiful creeper!' No one acknowledged the remark. We were waiting for the train for our return journey when madam suddenly said, 'Everything needs support, isn't it?' I could not make out whether it was an observation, a rhetorical question or an existentialist conclusion. Her eyes became misty and distant. Choked. I felt as if someone had hurled me from the top of a cliff. She is like that. Either she will make pointed observations or just clam up. She's either very relaxed and open or inexplicably tight-lipped.

Madam is ambling closer. She is just few steps away, spouting instructions to my neighbour. Certainly, she is walking up to my table. I have extracted the digestive system and cleaned up the frog. 'Now for cerebral system — upturn the frog on his stomach with his back facing you. Break the cerebral bone and the big and small brain of the frog becomes visible.' Saying this she walks over to another table. When she is not speaking, she appears to be deliberately pursing her lips together. The upper canine teeth are a little crooked and jut out. Of course, it is not visible externally but it gives her lips a pursed look.

A few drops fall on my only trousers while sipping tea at their house once. I was looking at madam and didn't see the drops falling but could feel it. Madam noticed the tea drops and said that the trousers needed a little sewing. 'Just a few stitches…give it, I'll mend it.' Did she really say these words? Doesn't matter, her eyes were saying 'Yes'. Her lips clammed up a little more tightly. Why is she so tight lipped? Sometimes she talks a lot; suddenly she withdraws into her shell, not allowing even Tina to break through. Why should she be so anxious and worried? I feel a little uneasy when she suddenly turns silent. I then converse with Tina for some time and then leave. I do not feel like coming back. But then she reminds me that Tina remembers me and I keep on coming back. 'Get well Tina!' I keep on telling her. Is there something wrong with madam as well?

Madam's mother was leaving by train that night. There was a lot of luggage. Madam did not ask me to wait and help but I did anyway. I stayed back, had food at their home and accompanied them to the railway station. I helped her stow away the luggage. Although it was heavily crowded, her mother got a place to sit. Once the train left the platform we hired a rickshaw and returned home. 'Okay, see you,' I said after escorting her to the door.

'Tina has fever. Can you wait tonight? I will wake you up early in the morning.' I did not say anything. Simply followed her in. I did not expect madam to ask me to stay on. Tina was fast asleep so she prepared two cups of coffee and talked animatedly for quite some time – mostly about her college days. It was rare to see her talk so cheerfully. Suddenly she became quiet, tears started rolling down, and she uttered a stifled, moaning sound, hiding her face in both hands. I didn't know what to do and was pinned down to my chair. However, she recovered fast, wiped her eyes, gave me a pillow and bedsheet and went into her room without a word. Her eyes had become cold. When she came to wake me up in the morning, I was already awake and ready to leave.

Gingerly, I break the frog's skull. Once the hard cover is removed, the brain is seen – it is a mass of spongy veins. Carefully, I clear the surrounding area. The brain becomes more visible. Madam is approaching. She bends to have a better look at the brain. As she bends, the pallu of her sari slips a little, her cleavage becomes visible. My hands tremble and the needle goes straight into the small brain damaging it completely.

Every passing hour makes the day shorter. The night is young and boring. My footsteps are lazy and drag me towards the hostel. I don't feel like going back to an empty room. Why do people return to their homes? Why don't they wait and listen to music, drink tea or beer and talk and laugh and shout and make merry. Every hour is a difficult hour. I feel like listening to unending music of love and life. Slowly tables start emptying. There are not many on the streets. I have to return to my room. What next?

A new day dawns, lingers on for some time ultimately ending into the night and I return to my room. All this gossip and talk is useless, meaningless – girls, teacher's muster, notebooks, dirty mess, new films and so on. Unending gossip. Sleep is evasive and I stand in the balcony. The gulmohar looks different at night. Different shapes invested with new feelings. In broad daylight it is more friendly and simple. At night it becomes ominous, and threatening. Just keep on walking up and down the corridor.

Finally, I get tired and return to the room, lock the door and switch off the light. Even then it is not dark. Moonlight keeps peeping through the half-closed window. It is neither properly lit nor pitch dark. Shadows on the wall keep on dancing as the gulmohar keeps swinging to and fro making the rays of light dance with it. The entire day passes before my eyes like an open frog ready for dissection. The events ricochet around my head making me dizzy. The night starts throwing its spell like a woman blowing a conch, in a trance-like state, beseeching divine power.

The crate of milk bottles clink sharply as the milk van arrives. Rakhma is sweeping the hostel grounds, her nipples feed her child, loud songs in the bathroom, deafening chatter in the classroom. I get out and look at the various faces, numerous movements of eyes, students gulping the tasteless food in the mess, the sly smile on Damager's face, the calm Irani counting change with dead fingers, becoming restless waiting for the next bill.

'Will you come for a movie?', 'Which one?', 'XYZ, they say it is good one', 'Taking notes will be useful for examinations', madam's observant gaze, spilling tea on my trousers, Tina and her evergreen smile, 'Come let us play, come on baby', the red glittering eyes of Tina's teddy, madam's delicate skilful fingers, very talkative, loosely held mane by a small ribbon, tightly closed crooked lips, 'Why do you cry, madam? Just tell me once, cry loudly. There is a small black mole on your back, you may not know it exists but I saw it once, did not tell you. It's like a small dot drawn by a needle. It appears round from a distance but as you close in you realize how many layers it has and it is no more black but different shades of grey, like a big blot with lots of sharp edges on a blotting paper, lonely, screwed, giving you deadly insomnia.'

Mother sitting amidst arranged luggage in the railway compartment, very naïve, 'What's there in the window, Tina?', 'Want to go out', 'Come just hold my finger', 'Keep quiet you idiots, what are you gossiping about?', Irani with

71

big beer belly, millions of known and unknown faces, where is the Damager's wife?, 'Rakhme, Oye Rakhme, sweep it clean, make it bright like your boobs', 'Come on, let's go to a movie', fire in the belly, decaying smell, dead fingers, uneasy fingers, skilful fingers, suspicious look, staring at the sky, shapeless shape, mom's illness in scribbled handwriting, millions of footsteps, at least take one, staring out of the window, curved crooked lips closing in, a loose bun, unending flow of warm tears rolling down on my shoulder.

I closed my eyes. My senses were numbed; my inner self was tired and weary and I removed the thoughts one by one, remove the hand below my head and sleep in such a manner that no part of my own body touches me. I'm in a state of senseless awareness and the feeling of touch is not leaving me. I'm lying prostrate with my back on the bed. I turn upside down on my stomach, gently and lightly becoming weightless and senseless, layers of touch are vaporizing, leaving the world of cognizance, entering into subtlety, heading straight into the womb.

'What's this?' madam says in a sad tone, 'Why are you rushing?'

Feeling awkward, I asked, 'Now what?' I look into her eyes.

The needle has entered straight into the brain.

I have never felt the pulse of a woman, but what finally remain are entangled, coagulated capillaries, broken muscles and disorganized organs.

Just Two Words

'ANNA EXPIRED!'

Absolutely numb, he kept gaping at the letter in his hand. He just couldn't believe it. The letter was short, only four-five lines. It had become dark but he did not light the lamp.

He was quite uneasy. He kept the letter on the table, sat on the cot, got up, opened the window, sat down again...He removed his shirt and felt a little better. But he was unable to come back to his senses. He could see just two words: 'Anna expired!'

He had been lying down on the cot for quite a long time

with his eyes closed. Absolutely still. He could hear the traffic outside, vehicles moving at a high speed with ear-piercing noise. Feeling dizzy, he opened the door and stepped out. The glitter on the road was unbearably bright. Resting his hands on the railing, he stood there for quite a long time. Vehicles, people, bicycles, cars were moving to and fro. His eyes did not take in anything clearly. The bright red letters on the signboard on the other side of the street appeared hazy and unclear.

The sky above was pitch dark. What was that? Nothing. But he looked at it intently. His hands were numb. Pulling himself away from the balcony, he went inside. He lit the lamp and wore the shirt that he had kept on the cot. He then put on his chappals. Locking the room, he went down. Nana, who was on the counter, smiled at him but he went straight out.

He wondered whether Ravi had come and immediately headed in that direction. Where else to go? In any emergency, Ravi is the only solution.

No one was in the drawing room. 'Is Ravi at home?' he called out.

Aunty came out.

'Oh hello dear! When did you come? Ravi hasn't yet come in but he should be here soon. Wait for him.'

He reclined on the cot. What to do sitting here? For how much time? For what? He must get ready to leave for Murtijapur. What about his leave? Let's see. Salary has not yet got transferred. When to start? Gosh! How fast is the second-hand moving! Tick, tick, tick…

Just then a bicycle was heard outside.

'Lo! Ravi is here!' called aunty from inside. 'You were asking for him and here he is – what a coincidence! May you live for a hundred years!'

The letter in the pocket pierced him – Who has seen hundred years?

'Hi Vikas! How are you? Oh, this bicycle! Got punctured on my way home. So, got late.'

He was quiet. Bicycle was rested against the wall.

'Mom, will you please prepare two cups of first-class tea? Is there anything to eat? I'm very hungry. Yes Vikas, what's up?'

Ravi's question was the usual one but the answer wasn't an expected one. He couldn't control himself and broke down.

'Oh dear! What happened?'

'Anna expired!'

'What? When?'

He wiped his tears and gave the letter to Ravi. Aunty kept all her work aside and came out.

'What did you say? Who has expired?'

'Vikas's Anna.'

'Oh god! Was he unwell?'

'No.'

'Then what must have happened all of a sudden?'

'I don't have any idea!'

'Who was Anna?'

'Vikas's grandpa,' explained Ravi.

'Mom's dad or father's?'

'Father's.'

'Okay. But who stays at Murtijapur?'

'He was staying alone.'

'Oh god! Are you leaving for your home?'

'What will I do going home? All will be at Murtijapur.'

Ravi's father came to the room.

'Yes Vikas, how are you?'

'His grandpa expired!' said aunty.

'Oh no! When?'

'Day before yesterday,' said Ravi.

'Are you going there?'

'Yes. Tonight. By the Nagpur Express.'

'Will your leave be sanctioned?'

'Hopefully.'

'Then have your dinner here only, and then go directly to the station.'

'I am not feeling hungry.'

'Don't say that. Eat something before you go. You know journeys are unpredictable.'

Aunty set the plates. He washed his hands, feet and face and both boys sat down and had a warm, nourishing dinner.

As he walked out, Ravi's father enquired whether he had enough money. He nodded affirmatively.

On way to Vikas's house, both were quiet. Roads were cooling down. Ravi quickly took out some clothes, hand-kerchief, towel, toothbrush, toothpaste and packed his bag.

'Please deliver this letter tomorrow to my office and this

receipt. Some clothes need to be brought back from the laundry. Here take this money. Come, let's move or I'll miss the train.'

The train wasn't crowded. He got a seat to sit but was still quite uneasy.

'Ravi.'

'Yes?'

'I couldn't meet Sushma today. Will you call her up tomorrow? Tell her I had to go home. It may take eight to fifteen days. I'll send her a letter. But please call her up.'

'Yes, sure. I'll call her up.'

There was still some time for the train to leave.

'Ravi, please give me a cigarette.'

'Oh no! I don't have one. Shall I get it? Wait. I will get a pack.'

Ravi came back in a few minutes and pressed a packet of Charminar into his hand. After three-four puffs, he felt better. The whistle blew. Ravi got down. 'Please don't forget about the phone,' he shouted.

He didn't even realize when the tonga arrived in front of the house. His eyes were tired. Everything was at its place but still something was amiss. The door was open. Before he could enter, his dad appeared in front of him from the kitchen garden. He felt as if his father had aged by ten years. His face was sullen and he had tied a thin towel round his head.

By the time he kept his bag down, everyone gathered in the veranda. Mom, aunty, siblings, cousins, nephews. No one could control their tears. His eyes were dry.

'Wash your hands and feet. Someone please prepare tea for him,' said his father and under the pretext of blowing his nose, wiped his tears.

He took water to wash his feet in the bathroom. Venu came in front of him with a vessel in her hand. He couldn't understand whether she was smiling or crying. He felt much better after drinking the smoky tea sitting on the cotton bedding. Next to the hearth was kept a brass cup and saucer. It was Anna's favourite. He would make a 'furr-furr' sound while drinking the tea. He would then wipe his moustache with the side of his dhoti and wearing chappals he would briskly…

'Has your leave been sanctioned?'

'I've sent a letter.'

'I suppose you will be able to stay back here for some days?'

'Yes. But how come all of a sudden?'

'Heart attack. Good that our neighbour Sawant was here. He immediately called for a doctor and telegrammed us. At least we could see him before the end.'

'But who was with him?'

'Who will be there? It was evening so Sawant was at home. Sheer stubbornness! Your father had requested him so many times to come and stay with us. I too have sent him at least four or five letters asking him to come to stay with us. But he didn't budge. Old age. It's not good to stay alone. We have a house here. We can follow all kinds of religious observances here as well. But he didn't ever want to hear a word about leaving Murtijapur. What will everyone think about us?' Tears flowed from mom's eyes.

'The firewood seems to be damp,' he said while staring at the smoke.

'Yes. He said that they are dry but doesn't seem so.'

'You are looking very pale, Vikas.' That was his aunt.

'Really?'

'What do you mean by "really"? Just look at the way you have lost weight. Don't you eat anything?'

'Yes,' said his mother. 'What to do? You know he is staying at the lodge and eats at odd times. These days...these children! Do you think they listen to us?'

He kept aside the cup and saucer and went out. Everything was in its place – the gulmohar trees, the half-fallen wall of the opposite house, the tall cupboard in the drawing room, the soiled carpet, the huge swing in the veranda. Sitting on the swing, he finally got a sense of belonging, the feeling of coming to the ancestral home.

'Vikas!' His father called out.

'Yes dad!'

'Will you please get the vegetables from the market first? And then go to take your bath.'

'Okay.'

The roads were empty. Muddy. He walked on the netted mosaic of footpaths past mud houses in various stages of repair, past coated plastered walls. There were hardly any passers-by. The entire village was calm and quiet. Everything at ease. He returned home with vegetables.

'Vikas, I suppose you are going to take your bath!' asked aunty in a loud voice.

'Yes.'

'Do you require hot water?'

'No. It's okay. I will have a cold water bath.' Taking off his shirt, he went to the well.

'Dad has gone to the post office. I too need to write a letter to Sushma,' he reminded himself. It will be the first time he will be writing a letter to her. What to write? How to start? Suddenly he stopped and smiled. He had brought only the rope to the well.

Venu was entering the yard and he called her.

'Will you please bring a bucket for me?'

'Smallie or biggie?'

'A big one.'

'Why not a small one?' She giggled as she ran, covering her mouth with the pallu of her sari. Venu was the same. Naughty and hard-working. The only change in her was that she had grown. He felt intensely that everything here was the same except in age. 'What do I write in the letter to Sushma? When I am returning or by which train! No. It's okay. Details later. Let me write in a poetic manner.'

Venu banged the bucket.

'Oye, you still thinking about this?'

He laughed.

'Venu, you're still the same!'

'Same…how?'

'Same means as you were.'

He kept the soap case next to a huge rock that had grown smooth over the years. He couldn't tie the knot of the rope properly. The sound of the bucket hitting the water was heard.

'Anna sahib, good person. Always observed religious rituals. Always helped the needy. When Chandu was ill, he helped us with medicine.'

Venu went on talking. He managed to drag the bucket up.

'He loved you much. Always used to remember – my Vikasbabu, my Vikasbabu.'

He lost control over the rope. Venu ran at once. Muttering 'Oh god!' she caught hold of the tail end of the rope behind him. Both of them were pulled forward. She instinctively fixed her one leg against the wall of the well. He felt shy and bewildered and came out of her arms. She pulled out the bucket – he kept staring at the movement of her hands.

'Here…take.' He was baffled.

She poured water from the bucket into the ghangaal – a large, circular metal vessel with handles. The rope had peeled off the skin from his palms while slipping from his hands. Venu saw his hands and asked, 'Blood?' rubbing his hands with her rough fingers.

Saying 'No, no,' he pulled the ghangaal. Drawing one more bucket of water, she went and sat on a boulder nearby. She sat in such a way that he could not see her face. He removed the rest of his clothes. She was sitting quietly.

'Venu.'

'Yes?'

'I hope you haven't got hurt!'

81

Saying 'No' she got up, kept the bucket in front of him and left.

He kept gazing at her back. The area surrounding the well was peaceful and quiet. He went on pouring water on himself. While trying to pull back the slipping rope, he was fully into her arms. Her warm breath had rested on his neck for some time. The fixing of her leg against the wall of the well had brought her closer. He felt better after taking a bath.

Plates for lunch were set in the huge passage that was at the centre of the house. The leafy vegetable curry cooked that day was his favourite. Anna loved it. Hardly anyone spoke while eating.

Priests came and performed the last rites and rituals, chanting mantras. He didn't believe much in it. He went to the attic, spread a mat and slept. Several events, incidences, memories flitted across his mind like a movie. He drifted into sleep with his memories bubbling till they overflowed.

He got up when Venu called him.

'Your mother is calling for you.'

He raised his eyebrows at her in a questioning manner. Venu was peeking through the door.

'Tea is ready. Your mother is calling you to come and have it.'

He quickly rinsed his mouth, went down and sat in front of his mother.

'Venu, please wash a cup and bring it.'

His mom, aunty and the lady from next door resumed their conversation.

'Do you remember?'

'What?'

'That Venu had first come here when Vikas was small.'

'Oh yes, yes, I remember. When you had come for your delivery during Nitin's time. Right?'

'Vikas was playing. A bright yellow snake came towards him. Venu noticed it. She risked her life, lifted him up and took him aside. Thank god! He was saved!'

He was looking at the firewood that wasn't burning. Venu put down the cup and went to bring the flour. The one who held his hand and took him around to see the fair when he was young was none other than Venu, she used to pluck guavas for him, told fairy tales, looked after Anna and all his ailments, worked like mad during aunty's marriage, helped mom during her delivery. Venu grew up working at Anna's place. She got married and continued working at Anna's place. When her husband died, she took another job at some other place but continued to do all the work at Anna's place. Ask for anything and Venu was always ready!

Feeling an impulse to smoke a cigarette, he put on his shirt and went out. With Anna he had never missed any visits to the temples. He came back after his smoke without going very far. It darkens very early in the village and there were no known acquaintances. Everyone was awake at home till late night. He applied oil on his hands and went off to sleep.

The next morning, he woke up early to the chanting of mantras. Some discussion was going on between a close friend of Anna and his father regarding the last rites and rituals. He went to the bathroom and rinsed his mouth. Venu was engrossed in washing utensils. He stepped on the veranda with a cup of tea when a tonga was heard approaching the house.

Prabha aunty had arrived. Her eyes were filled with tears and by the time she climbed the steps to the veranda, she broke down. His mom, aunt, cousins rushed in to console her. Dad stayed where he was. He didn't have the courage to move. Anna's close friend, Dadasahib, went ahead and brought her in. Unloading the luggage from the tonga, Vikas kept it in the veranda and escaped to the attic. He felt depressed when he saw elderly people crying. Tears didn't well up in his eyes. Crying every time a new person arrives is not good. He cried at Ravi's house – that was it. After that he didn't cry at all. He could see his father was very tired and took the responsibility of going to the market for buying the things that were needed. To and fro – continuous errands.

It was quite late when he got the time to bathe. Taking a small bucket and rope, he went to the well. Venu was there filling her pitcher.

'Give it to me. I'll draw the water.'

'No. It's okay. I can do it.'

'Oh? Else like yesterday!'

'I got a small bucket today.'

'So what?' There was naughtiness in her eyes as she took the bucket from his hands and drew up water.

'Did you apply anything on your hands?'

'Yes. Oil.'

'What oil? Apply some ointment.'

After lunch he went off to sleep. He didn't hear Venu's wake-up call and she came in. She held his shoulders and shook him till he woke up.

In the evening when he came back from another market errand, he managed to save himself from tumbling over on Venu.

'Look and walk properly. Why are you pushing me?' In the fumble, his arms were caught in her hands. Venu's eyes glittered in the darkness. He came inside without speaking a word. With a single touch, he sensed Venu trickling down like mercury.

Days passed by doing market errands and talking. The number of people visiting the house also increased and so did his errands. Vessels and groceries were constantly falling short.

'Vikas, please help Venu to draw water from the well. Poor thing gets tired! Both of you draw and your aunts will bring it in and pour,' called out his father. Since a big bucket was attached to the rope, it was taking less time to draw water. One hand for pulling the rope was his, the next was hers. Within a few seconds, the bucket was up.

'Don't leave the rope like the other day.'

'No. Anyway, now you are there to help me, isn't it?'

Venu was happy. She was trying to be meddlesome and unnecessarily asking about this or that, trying hard to grab his attention.

His mother announced: 'Rice needs to be cooked in a bigger degh (a metallic vessel with a bigger base and narrow mouth).'

'What should I do?' His father was clearly annoyed.

'I have one degh with a big base on the loft,' piped in Venu. 'I just need someone with me to get it down.'

'Should I come?' asked his father in a lacklustre tone.

'No. It's okay,' said his mother. 'You be here. Look after the cooks who are going to come. Vikas, you go along with her and get that degh.'

He didn't want to go at all but knew arguing wouldn't help him.

It was very hot outside. The roads were silent and empty.

'Vikasbabu, can I ask you one thing?'

'Yes. Ask.'

'When are you going to get sweets for us?'

'For what?'

'Your wedding, of course!'

'Oh! No, no, not so early. There is still much time.'

'Will you invite me?'

'Obviously! Without you –'

'This way.' That lane led directly to her house. It was afternoon. The mill workers were at work and the lane was as sluggish as a corpse. The door to her cottage was ajar. He followed her inside.

'Here. You will need to climb,' she said and pulled a mortar from behind her. The wall of the house was made of straw and bamboo, plastered with mud and cow dung. There was a loft over one area. He held the mortar tightly. When she stepped on it, it tottered. Her thigh rubbed against his cheek. The moment she kept her second leg on it, the mortar slipped and she tumbled down.

While trying to help her from falling down, the touch had become quite intimate. She became stable. His breath had become warm. He strengthened the grip on her shoulders. Her hands went behind him and pulled him towards her. He didn't know when his lips had touched her thick and fuller lips. Venu could sense the increasing passion in his fingers.

A wind struck against the door, banging it. He pushed himself away from her. It became difficult to control her impulse. Venu wiped the sweat on her face. He avoided the call in her eyes.

'Hold it,' he told her, gesturing at the mortar. He stepped on it and quickly brought down the degh.

'Tea?'

'No.'

'Why? When young, you did not move without having a cup of tea. But now who belongs to you here? Once you go, you won't come back. When Anna was alive, you came. Why would you come now?'

'No, nothing as such. It's already late. Mom must be waiting', he said and walked out with the degh. When she took Anna's name he instantly loathed her.

The Thirteenth Day – the day of Hindu funeral rites and rituals after death – was just two days away. The hustle and bustle increased. Venu toiled hard. Whenever she could, she would appear in front of him, ask if he needed anything. While drawing water she would touch him intentionally. Evading everyone's eyes, she would glare at him.

He developed a sort of repugnance towards her. He didn't want to see her anywhere close to him. In the afternoon when she shook him to wake him up, he at once got annoyed and told her, 'Why are troubling me again and again? Let me sleep.' From the next day she did not come to wake him up. In spite of not wanting to draw water with her, that was something he had to continue.

The Thirteenth Day was over and all those who had come started leaving one by one. His parents were staying back for a few more days to complete all the final transactions. He was leaving with his uncle and aunt. He did not have any more leave and the table tennis matches were also nearing.

What he didn't feel in those twelve days, he felt it while leaving. Tears froze in his dry eyes. He bent down in obeisance to everyone – Dadasahib, Sawant uncle, the next-door lady and Venu, who was standing behind the pillar.

'I'm leaving, Venu.' She didn't speak anything. Tears were running down her cheeks. He shouldn't have snapped at her in such a harsh manner.

The tonga arrived at the gate. Everyone waved farewell till the tonga took a turn at the corner of the road. And after that Venu' eyes…

At the bus stand, he saw a post box. He had completely forgotten to write the letter to Sushma.

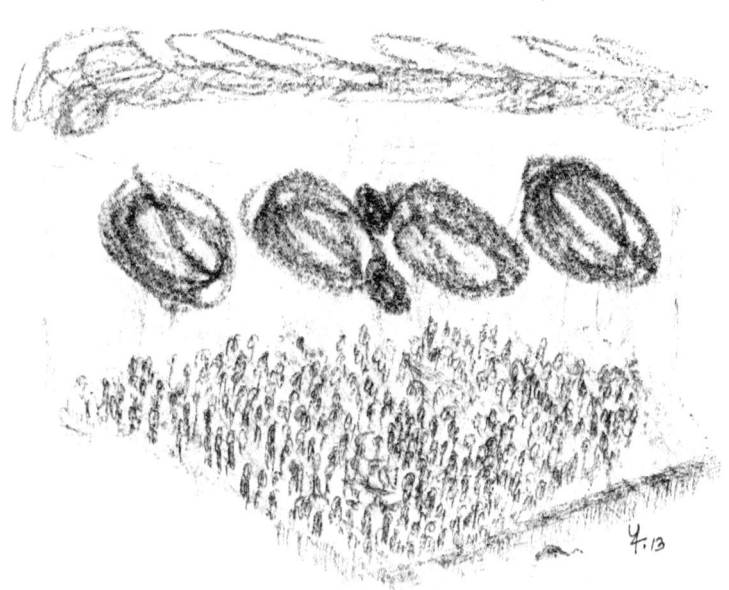

Four Zeros

THE INDICATOR ON THE PLATFORM was showing zero zero zero zero. Seeing those zeros, he chuckled.

Completely packed…commotion…who was talking with whom and saying what…couldn't understand a word. On both platforms, people were standing or moving about like ants.

The rain had stopped. It was wet and muddy everywhere. In the yellow light of the platform, everything was looking sick and yellow – yellow faces, yellow clothes, yellow chattering teeth, black hair shimmering yellow, yellow signals on both ends of the platform…not even green or red. Not a single train coming or going. In that yellowish darkness, the glimmer of the rail tracks also looked queer, like the two lines on someone's forehead – not leaving its silvery shine in that yellowish shade. Where were they going to lead? Wherever they led, following them would be of no use.

Zero zero zero zero.

Four zeros – that meant a complete standstill, no guarantee of anything. A loud scream signalling the complete collapse of the railway system. Two dots between those four zeros – glimmering – like the two eyes of an unknown omnipotent force observing the city. But why do we wait till the indicator shows four zeros?

The bag in his hand had also started to feel heavy. What was making it so full? An empty tiffin, an empty water bottle, a monthly railway pass, some papers, a document which had created a furore in the evening and a plastic bottle containing colourful tablets. Nothing else – oh but also the same glittering droplets spattered on the bag! It had been raining since so long that there was no trace of dryness. His hair, which had gradually grown sparse, had become wet, sticking to his forehead.

In the afternoon, a computer specialist had come to the office to deliver a two-hour lecture. He said that the computers in the entire world would face a huge problem. While explaining, he even drew four zeros. After the year 1999, on the first day of 2000, there would be a deadly snag in all the computers. Because the first two zeros had permanently been made 19. The next two zeros could change and continue till 99, but one could not type 2000. And then there would be utter confusion when a 00:00 day would dawn. Due to which the entire computer system was going to collapse. He said that everyone would face a 'major catastrophe'. That means the New Year would start with an incomprehensible question!

How long did one have to wait? When was this train going to come? Even when it came, it would be so crowded. Would he get a chance to get in? He desperately wanted to go home. He was completely exhausted. His legs ached – might fold anytime, like a folding chair. But getting a place to sit was next to impossible. The train arriving would be a crammed one, with only four-five people alighting, whereas fifteen-twenty people would try to board. Must somehow manage to squeeze in along with the bag. Once one had got in, one could get some space to stand. With a proper push from behind, it would be possible to make way. Such a big door, but it seemed to be a small one while getting in. If he could catch hold of the rod at the centre, then it would be possible to get in a bit easily – that too, if it were First Class. Second Class was absolutely impossible. The very thought of getting into a Second Class compartment made him shudder.

He took out his mobile phone from his shirt pocket. Thank god, the battery had not run out! At least water had not entered the phone. The moment he switched it on, all the figures popped up brightly. Dialled a number and within a few seconds, could get a call through. His wife picked up after two rings.

'Hello!'

Definitely the TV must be on – he initially imagined it, and then said, 'It's me. It's raining heavily. So the trains are late.'

'Yes, they reported it in the news.'

'Will be late. Have your dinner. Is Tinku back?'

'Yes.'

'And Pinki?'

'She also has come.'

'Okay.'

He disconnected the call and put the phone in his shirt pocket. His speech was so loud that it was easily audible in that commotion. In any case, anyone in such a situation attracts attention and is audible because the person seems to be talking loudly to himself. Like ripples that form on the water and subside within a few seconds, the curiosity of those who listened to him talking over the phone also subsided.

In that milling crowd, he took the support of his knee, opened his bag and took out a cigarette packet. Closed his bag, took out a cigarette, put it in his mouth, opened the bag again and put the cigarette packet back in. Took out the lighter from his pocket and lit the cigarette. Looking up, he released smoke in the air. The sky was dark and the drizzle was visible.

He had to go to office the next day because the zonal general manager had called for a meeting. His presence was not required at all. But since all the departmental GMs had been called, he had to go. Otherwise there wasn't any need to go to office in such heavy rain.

AFTER JOINING Mather and White, he didn't feel any need to change the company. After working for years in the stores department of the company, he had got a chance to work under many top-level officers and managers. While doing so, he had landed a plum position.

But for the past five years, he had constantly been feeling that there was something amiss. Many of his colleagues had left the company and joined elsewhere. Some of them had opted for voluntary retirement, got some five-ten lakhs and gone back to their native place. Policies changed. Many newcomers grabbed senior posts. A realization that his experience of so many years was proving futile began gnawing at him.

Initially, when the workers' union had objected to the use of computers, he was in a clerical post. Obviously, he too was involved in the protest against use of computers. Gradually, the protest subsided. Staunch opponents were transferred to the outposts. By the time computers were accepted almost everywhere, he had reached the executive level. And within a short time, he had reached the managerial level.

A droplet from nowhere landed on the tip of the cigarette. Before he could puff it, it got extinguished. The same way, no one knows from where, a drop fell and completely thawed his career. He had always stood first class first and had stupendous experience, but didn't realize when he stopped ascending the continuous ladder of promotion. No one had informed him about it either. Those ascending steps were gently sawed and separated. When he realized, he fumed with rage. He got some sympathy, but events were happening so fast that he didn't get time to ponder over matters.

Diwan, a highly qualified young lad with merely five years of experience and an extensive social network, had reached his level. Enviable credentials – age, qualifications, family background, recognition in the circle of the higher authorities, etc.

'You're lucky! New policies, new targets, new systems – it's surprising that you haven't got a golden handshake yet!' Diwan had once causally commented. This comment pierced him like an electric shock and he spent a year or two consoling himself.

It became mandatory for everyone to learn how to operate computers. Everything was so different. Unheard of words began to enter his ears. Slowly, he was pushed out of all the important departments and relegated to the least important ones.

The old furniture was replaced by new furniture, there was centralized air-conditioning and there were plastic flowers and posh cabins – within no time, the entire atmosphere and ambience had changed. But what to do sitting idle? He had a staff of fifteen under him – all fresh graduates who couldn't fit into that environment. Even they started decreasing in number. It was he who had to reduce the number. Without reason, sack them. How merciless! No scope for sympathy or compassion. But gradually, he got used to that as well. Ultimately one fine day, unable to control himself, he asked the regional manager, 'Sir, I have got a good staff. So apart from our work, if we could get some project planning…'

'Relax, man! How many years you have toiled on the field! I know it very well. Have patience. Else you will be shooting yourself in the foot. By the way, good that it is to me that you have spoken. Don't utter a word regarding this to anyone. Otherwise your entire department will be closed down with "unwanted" as a remark. So, chill.'

After that he didn't broach the topic. Earlier while coming into his cabin, he would read 'D.N. Vijapurkar, General Manager', and feel happy. But now it was more like, 'Do or don't do the work; whatever you have, do it. Just relax. No question of promotion at all. The only thing to take care of is that you shouldn't be sacked from the company.'

SUDDENLY, THE PUBLIC address system made a grating noise. Everyone became alert. His eyes, which were looking fixedly into nothing, fell on the indicator on the platform again. The globular shaped zeros were still standing erect.

After the morning lecture, 'new century' got fixed in his brain in such a way that he is visualizing and comparing every possible thing with the new century. How will this look, how will that look, will any changes take place – it is almost turning into a mania. 'The local (train) which is going to arrive will be transporting us from this era into the new century!' He chuckled at this thought. At other times, it wouldn't have been possible for him to chuckle or laugh in this manner, but in this dark rain, who had the time to look at his face, which was turning grey like the crowd! 'New century – new dreams.

Would our company return to normalcy? Surprising! Does that mean I am going into the next century or going back into the earlier one?'

He saw something moving on the gleaming rail tracks, but was unable to make out what it was. There wasn't any clarity – as if a part of the dark floating clouds had crumpled down. But when he strained his eyes, he saw some movement – oh, this is our rat! What is he doing on the rail tracks? Moving up and down the rail tracks, in and out of the burrow, twisting his tail, looking here and there, thrusting his neck down, and vanishing within seconds. And while scurrying, if raindrops fall, his flesh creeps. Is he also waiting for the new era?

Water had already entered his shoes and his socks were completely wet. Due to this, he was feeling very cold. Even while sitting in the air-conditioned room in office, he had never felt so cold. No trace of any train. The announcer must also be dozing in front of the mike waiting for the next era.

Among the crowd, he noticed an old woman with her legs folded close to her stomach. She was selling bananas and had one of her hands on the basket. The wrinkles on her face made it impossible to know whether her eyes were open or closed. Under that yellowish tinge, the green of the raw bananas was clearly visible.

'Surprising!' he muttered to himself, moving behind towards the pole. 'In such heavy rains, who is going to eat these bananas?' Though he asked himself this, looking at them he felt hungry. That wasn't the time to feel hungry. But maybe the rain and the long wait had something to do with it.

Before leaving the office, he had had grilled sandwiches as usual and even gulped down lemon tea without milk. Actually, he was not supposed to eat grilled sandwiches. Each time, the doctor told him, 'Watch your cholesterol' – just as grandpa used to tell him when he was young: 'My dear, be careful whenever and wherever you step.'

Now how to manage cholesterol? However much you try to control it, it goes on increasing. Partly to blame was Sakharam's grilled sandwich – absolutely incomparable – followed by lemon tea for officers and regular milk tea for others. Everyone in the office has become an officer. Even the youngest clerk had become an executive assistant. The company doesn't lose anything by making everyone an executive. With everyone becoming part of the management, there was no question of any kind of trade union activity in the company. Anyone could be sacked anytime – like the peeling off of a banana skin.

Taking shelter under the platform's shade, a completely drenched crow was cawing loudly on the electric wire. It flapped its wings and within a few seconds, flew away and disappeared. Isn't this cawing of the empty stomach?

His gaze again fell on that old woman and the drenched basket. Even the bananas must have become wet. But that old woman was sitting stoically with closed eyes, waiting for an unknown customer. Raw bananas could be sold tomorrow as well. Was there any obligation for her to sell them today itself? At that moment, she happened to open her eyes slightly and close them again. Maybe she wanted to convey, 'There is no obligation, but it's a matter of life and death. If these bananas are not sold, then what to eat?'

'Then eat bananas!'

The old woman opened her eyes again. Who was telling her to eat bananas? He felt awkward. Had he said, 'Then eat bananas!' aloud? He had fallen into the habit of talking to himself and in so doing, he would often blurt things out loud. He didn't remember when he had developed this habit. It was somewhat like the computer yelling, 'Are you crazy?' if you happened to press a wrong button. Listening again and again to the computer, he had started wondering whether he had become crazy too.

After working hard through the day when he put forth his leg, he would feel as if he was trudging with some heavy weight attached to his legs. It would become impossible to lift his leg and if lifted, it would become difficult to put it back. In the same way, he would talk to himself, especially while travelling in a crowded train, staring nowhere or thinking aloud.

Actually, he wouldn't have realized. But for the people who turned back to look at him, and he would come to his senses and wonder whether he had spoken aloud. 'Did I say, "Then eat bananas!" aloud?' The old woman did not look at him, but he felt awkward.

He noticed that two young lads had stopped in front of her. How did she get to know that they were going to come? Sensing them coming closer, she must have opened her eyes.

For no reason he felt awkward, as if it was because of his speaking aloud that she must have opened her eyes. The lads bought two bananas each and put the money in her hand. She took out the change that she kept in the wicker basket under the bananas and gave it to them. While waiting for the train, both of them stood on the edge of the platform, ate those bananas and hurled the banana peels on the rail tracks. One fell exactly at the spot where the rat was scurrying up and down, moving in and out of the burrow.

Sitting on that shining track, it looked intently at the banana peel that had fallen in front of it all of a sudden. After looking here and there ten-twelve times, it got down and moved a bit ahead. Gazed at it again. Found that it wasn't moving, went close to it and smelt it. Again, after some surveillance, it took the peel into its mouth and started dragging it backwards.

He could see all these happenings from the spot where he was standing. But he couldn't see whether the rat took the banana peel into its burrow or whether it left it on the tracks. Before dragging it, it had gnawed at it two or three times. It must have liked it; that's why it had made the effort to drag it along.

He had heard of lambs eating banana peels and had seen them doing so, but didn't know that even rats eat them. Surprisingly, the rats in this city did not spare even banana peels. Either the rat must not be getting anything to eat, or it might have got habituated to eating anything thrown down on the tracks. He also remembered reading somewhere that five kilograms of plastic had been extracted from a cow's stomach.

He knew he saw only one. But there must be plenty. Who cared or bothered to notice?

Till the time that rats don't gnaw at the rail tracks and trains don't get derailed, they are going to live freely. He felt such an intense desire to see what must have happened to the banana peel that he shoved his way through the crowd up to the side of the platform, but not to the edge. First of all, it was very clammy. And if by some chance he got even a slight push from behind, he would fall off the platform along with his attaché case and the rats would pounce on him and chew him up. One couldn't predict what they would be gnawing at and taking away by the time he could stand back.

The loudspeaker, the senses of which had been deadened, came alive all of a sudden. Everyone pricked up their ears. What would one be able to hear in such a commotion? The grating of the microphone got in the way of its audibility.

'This is Central Broadcasting Station...'

One could hear only this clearly, as if someone had spoken from the heavens. After that, nothing was audible. But one thing was clear – that the trains were going to be late for an indefinite period of time. Once again, there was activity on the platform. Some hurled abuses in irritation. Some sneered. Some walked out of the station.

His legs started aching as he had been standing continuously for a long time. He glanced around to see if there was any place to sit. All the seats were occupied.

It was impossible to get a taxi and even if he got one, they would definitely charge two-three hundred rupees. And anyway, even if he had been ready to shell out that amount, getting an empty taxi at that time was highly unlikely.

The intensity of the rain had lessened. Though it was drizzling, there wasn't any need to use an umbrella. What else to do? How much time to wait? How to kill time? With the expectation of finding an alternative, he tried to make his way out of the crowded station. But unfortunately, it was more crowded and bright outside, with a lot of razzmatazz. The opposite footpath and Udupi restaurant were equally crowded. All the shops had closed down; only the small booths and kiosks of eatables were open.

The neon signboards on the building on the opposite corner were flickering. Strings of small red, yellow and green bulbs were hanging on both sides – a permanent symbol of jubilation.

But where to sit? Even if he went to Udupi restaurant for some tea or coffee and happened to get a place to sit, he would have to get up once done, considering the crowd. So, it was better to avoid it. It seemed there was a bar at the corner. But even there, there was no guarantee of getting a place to sit. He thought that he should at least take a round and see if he could find a place to sit. If he got one, well and good. Else he would return. Couldn't read the letters from a distance. When he went closer, he could read.

Blue Gate.

Let it be whichever gate; at least after it opened there

would be some scope for sitting down and relaxing. A huge strapping gateman was standing at the entrance. As he approached, the man slowly opened the door. Inside, there was a young lad wearing a coat, perhaps the maître d'. Seeing that there was no one else with him, the young man took out a small notepad and asked, 'One?'

He nodded.

'Come.'

There was more commotion inside – clouds of smoke, lights, a huge chandelier, people, waiters, manager...He followed the lad. From the room that looked like a hall, he was ushered into an inner dark room, which also seemed to be packed with people. It looked as if they were completely drenched in that darkness.

Saying, 'Please come,' the young man opened a door at the corner, led him in and closed it behind him, and then escorted him to another hall upstairs. It was bigger, with more light. All the tables were occupied. In one corner, there was a single table with a single person occupying it. The maître d' pointed it out to him, holding the notepad in his hand. He said, 'Sorry sir, but that is the only seat vacant.' He didn't utter a word and put his attaché case beside him. The person sitting across him did not even take heed of him. Must have been sitting there for a long time. He was tired and bored, and felt desperately like getting back home. But he must kill time.

'Please place the order or else it will be too late.'

'What is available?'

The waiter, who had suddenly appeared, threw a menu

card in front of him. He picked it up and went through it. By the time he looked up to place the order, the young man who had ushered him in and the waiter who had come to take the order had both vanished. He realized that the fat person sitting opposite him was staring slyly at him. At that moment, he felt he had seen those fatigued eyes – which looked like glass beads – somewhere. But he couldn't recollect.

Behind the fat person was a huge digital wall clock that showed 22:30. It made him reflect on how he had wasted those two hours on the platform. Feeling uneasy, he desperately looked around for the waiter. No one came to his table. The person across him, without moving even a single muscle on his face, was still staring at him continuously. The table was empty – not even a glass, spiced groundnuts or ashtray. Had he placed an order or was he, like himself, waiting for the waiter?

The table beside him was also empty – no glass, no ashtray, nothing! People were only chatting with each other. The waiters were moving around hurriedly with empty trays. Initially, there was enough light, but now everything was becoming darker. Even the face of the person across was turning dark. Only the wristwatch was shining with prominence.

00:00

'What?' Even the wall clock opposite him had stopped!

'The lights have gone off,' the person across said, as if from within a deep cave. He broke out into a sweat. From his forehead, the sweat trickled onto his cheek. In order to call up home, he hastily took out his phone. The screen gleamed, 'Out of range.'

He kept on asking, 'Where am I?'

Box of Sweets

H E ASKED WHILE PUTTING DOWN HIS BAG, 'Do you have a room?'

A young lad, sporting a vest and a newly sprouted moustache, was so engrossed in the register that it seemed doubtful whether he had seen or heard him making the enquiry. Finally, he curtly closed the two-foot-long register and spoke without even looking up.

It was obviously annoying. He always felt the same way when anybody treated him with disdain.

After a long and tiring day of drudgery, he was so exhausted that he desperately wanted a place to lie down. In addition, commuting in and around the village was not at all comfortable. There was no autorickshaw or taxi on the road. The only mode of transport available from the factory to the village was a bus, which came every one or two hours.

Walking down wasn't a big deal, but he didn't have any energy left in him. Moreover, the stray dogs on the farm would attack any unknown face. Long ago, a mechanic who had come to repair the company's boiler had started walking towards the village. On his way, a dog had attacked him and bit his calf, and he had to take fourteen rabies injections. As if this was not enough, several cases of robbery had also been reported. As an alternative, there was a guest house at the factory. But since there was a 'Farmer's Entrepreneurial Exhibition' going on, all the rooms were booked. Some VIPs were going to visit the factory, so there was a lot of hustle and bustle.

Actually he had decided to return home after finishing the day's work. But Jadhav sir had vanished after lunch and reappeared only at four-thirty – must have come after taking a good nap. And he had to sit on the steel chair and wait for him. The heat was unbearable. Who else could have given him the files? The worst part was that some person or the other would occasionally peek in and ask, 'Is Jadhav sir there?' It was like rubbing salt in the wound when he himself was waiting for Jadhav sir. When he got tired of saying 'No,' he turned many of them back by shaking his head in reply. This started making his neck ache.

'I HOPE YOU ARE IN no hurry to go back,' said Jadhav sir. 'Stay back tonight. Since we will have guests tomorrow, I will be occupied but our work won't be held up. Mrs Tayde will provide you with whatever you need...Wait, I'll introduce you to her.'

Jadhav sir rang the bell.

No one came. So he rang the bell again. A peon came and knocked on the door.

'Yes, sir!'

'Where were you? How many times have I got to ring the bell! Go at once and call Mrs Tayde.'

'Okay, sir.'

'Mrs Tayde, this is our new Deputy Circle Officer. I'll be a little busy with the function. Please provide him with the necessary files he requires. Ask him if he needs anything else and help him out.'

'Yes, sir.' Mrs Tayde left without waiting for another moment.

'There's a small problem.'

'What's that?'

'You see, our guest house is completely full. So, we've made arrangements for you to stay at Hotel Chandralok. It's a good hotel, but not as good as the ones in your city. Kindly excuse us if you feel uncomfortable. I'll be there in the evening to see to the arrangements made for you.' Jadhav sir went on talking while searching for some paper.

'It's okay. Not necessary...'

'No, no. How come you are saying "it's not necessary"? It's

very much necessary. It's our sahib's order. We must ensure that you have a nice, comfortable stay.

'You will have to go by bus. We could have sent a car for you, but there is a slight hitch. These days we are observing a code of conduct. Tomorrow, one of our higher authorities is going to visit. We have made completely personal and private arrangements for him. You see if we do it any other way, we will get into trouble. I will make some arrangements to show you the bus stop.'

Even though he said 'No', Jadhav sir asked a peon to accompany him. Instead, from the door itself, the peon pointed to a banyan tree outside the compound. There was a small booth and a banana seller sitting nearby. That was the bus stop.

It seemed as if the factory staff left immediately after him. Most of them stood in clusters near the bus stop. Mrs Tayde was among the group of ladies. The bus arrived after half an hour. It resembled a school bus. What a mess, commotion and clamour followed!

CHANDRALOK WAS ON THE OUTSKIRTS of the village. So he was the first person to get off.

At the hotel, after writing his name and address in the register, he pushed it towards the young lad. Sensing something, the young lad asked, 'Have you come through Jadhav sir?'

'Yes, had some work at the factory.'

'Then why didn't you tell me earlier? He has already

booked a room for you.'

'It's okay. Now book a room for me in my name.'

'I know. I can understand. But since sir has instructed us, we must listen to him. By the way, the room will be booked in your name only. If you want, I will also prepare a bill in your name. But I must give you the room which sir has asked me to give you. You are our guest.'

Before he could say anything further, the young lad rang the bell and called the room boy and gave him the keys. 'Show sir the room. Have you cleaned and arranged it properly? He is Jadhav sir's guest. Provide him with hot water.'

The special room was on the second floor. But climbing the steep staircase was a difficult task. Finally, his corner room was opened. The room boy opened the windows. A particular stink was pervading the stuffy room. There was a big double bed. The cover on it might have been washed, but looked dirty. A dirty water-jug. A glass. A small TV set in the corner. When he pressed the button, the images moved up and down, and he could hear a grating sound. It was a typical, old eight-channel cable TV set. He tried changing the channel to some music channel. But there too the grating sound was louder than the songs.

'If you require anything, then ring the bell. The telephone isn't working.'

'Okay.'

He took off his shirt and kept lying for quite a long time.

He rang the bell and called the room boy, and asked for a bucket of hot water and tea. He had a bath and sat on his bed.

He noticed a packet of mosquito coils.

He tried watching TV, but the grating sound was too irritating. The pictures were continuously moving up and down. He tried making them still, but in vain.

Touring is exasperating! Killing time in the evening is the worst part of it. He thought of taking a stroll around the hotel and then having an early dinner before going to sleep. Someone knocked on the door. Thinking it was the room service boy, he shouted, 'Come in. The door is open.'

Jadhav sir entered the room.

'Come in. Come in.'

'I'm sorry I came to your hotel room directly from the factory, without giving you a warning. Sahib has sent me a message that he is at the bungalow. If you don't mind, could we go and meet him?'

'Yes. No problem. Let's go.'

They went to the bungalow. It was buzzing with activity. People going in, people coming out. They were served coffee and biscuits. Sahib did not have much time since he had to go out somewhere. His bungalow was slightly out of the village, about a kilometre ahead of Chandralok. There was a river flowing from behind his bungalow.

He came to the topic directly. 'Sahib, we have faced a lot of problems while setting up this factory. It's functioning smoothly. You must have noticed the change. But there is a lot of politics. Wild allegations are being made against us. We need the loan desperately. If we don't get the loan, then we might have to shut down the factory. One thousand twelve hundred people will become jobless. Our farmers will be ruined. Everything will go haywire.'

Sahib didn't give him a chance to speak at all. He was like a school student sitting in front of Sahib.

Sahib spoke so fast that he couldn't even say, 'Okay, I'll look into it.' But he got the gist of what Sahib was saying. Sahib spoke in a measured way, but to the point. He put forth his case without mincing words. But at the same time, he was paying him due respect. He just could not imagine such an influential, wealthy person pleading with him for help and talking in such a down-to-earth manner.

'Jadhav, look after sir in every way. Where are you staying? I know they have started troubling you. People are suffering for no rhyme or reason. But what do we do? Our hands are tied. It's okay. Jadhav will explain everything to you. In fact, he will keep everything ready for you. You only need to give us the permission. There should not be any problem. I will take care of everything. The regional officer is coming down next week. He pays a visit to the deity once in a while. We are lucky that he takes care of our problems. You also visit us. So shall I take your leave now? Jadhav, take good care of him. See to it that there is no shortage of anything.'

Saying this, Sahib got up, joined his hands in salute, sat in his car and left.

AFTER REACHING THE HOTEL ROOM, saying 'I'll be back', Jadhav sir went down. He returned with a brown packet and a box.

'Sahib has given this for you. We get wonderful sweetmeats over here. And this is the report. I have prepared it along with him. All the figures in this are perfect. Everything is tallying. You need not bother. Also, if you wish, you can go back by the early morning train. Else you can go through the report. But you will be wasting your time unnecessarily. That's all.' Saying this, Jadhav sir gave a shrewd smile.

'Would these people allow me to say anything? Or do they take everything for granted?' He wondered and put the brown envelope and the box of sweets on the table.

'Please feel free to ask me for anything. Shall I take your leave? If you have any problem, please feel free to call up. You have my number…right?' Saying this, Jadhav sir hurried out.

He sat quietly for two minutes. Switched on the fan and the TV. Went through the report that Jadhav sir had got typed…It was exactly as it should have been. So much so that only some space was kept vacant for his signature.

He kept staring at the report, wondering about the contents of the box.

Dad and the Interview

THE REPORTER IS BUSY PREPARING himself with a set of questions for the interview. He takes out a notebook and pen from his pocket.

'Congratulations.'

'Thank you.'

The reporter looks at his notebook. Then looks at him again. Grins. He smiles back.

He is sitting on one corner of the bed with legs crossed, in a relaxed manner.

For some time, the reporter looks at the notebook. Then looks at him again. Grins. But this time, the student does not acknowledge his grin…

Now he has to start the interview. But how to begin?

The reporter always gets restless, especially before taking an interview. But once he gets started, there is no stopping him. He goes on expanding the interlinked questions.

'What were your feelings when you learnt that your dad had been appointed to the highest position?'

'I was happy.'

He writes it down – 'is happy'. He scribbles something. Draws lines. He is expecting the student to say something further. The reporter shifts his gaze from the pen and looks at the student, but is surprised to see him looking down at his own toes.

He reads those words – 'is happy' – again. Looks at his student again. But gets a feeling that there is no happiness reflected on the grim face of the student, who is still looking at his toes.

The first question is over. The next follows.

If this student stood up, he would be six feet tall. He looks tired but robust. His narrow head makes him look a bit immature. A bent nose – resembling that of his father in the photograph that appeared in the morning newspapers today. But why is this student looking so lost? He should be happy about his father's achievement.

In an attempt to break the ice, the reporter asks him, 'When did you hear of your father's appointment…?'

'Read it in today's morning newspaper. And when you called me up.'

'Oh! That means you didn't get to hear of this news earlier…'

'No.'

'Then what are your feelings since you read the news? Do you feel elated?' He realized that he was repeating the question – let's see…at least now he may give a detailed answer.

'Uh…Yes, I'm proud of it.'

Once again a long pause. It seems like he is searching for the right words to answer. His eyes keep moving from the ceiling…to the reporter…back to his toes, and then to the notebook.

The reporter waits – hopefully he will get some clear statements. But there is silence.

'How is your father?' Catches him at the moment when his eyes fall on the reporter…waits expectantly…At least now he will let out some information!

Still…silence.

'How is your father?' he asks again.

'How means…I didn't get you. What is it you want to ask?'

'I mean his nature, his behaviour, etc…'

'Nature?…He has always been kind and helpful. But a strict disciplinarian.'

'Okay. Then tell me when did you get to know that such a prestigious position had been conferred upon your father and what was your reaction?

'Was very happy. Felt proud.'

Before he looks back at his toes, the reporter asks the next question. 'Can you recall any memories of your dad?'

'Um…Aah…He was a very strict disciplinarian. He would always speak the truth and followed a strict schedule, that is, a particular time of waking up, having lunch, dinner, sleeping, and also expected everyone to follow the same.'

The reporter pretends to write something in his book but there is nothing important to write about. How to extract information? Why is he shying away from giving information on his dad? Sullen idiot.

'Let us know something about your father…'

'He was born in…'

His birth date, place of birth, his educational attainments when he joined the armed forces, medals, his bravery in the war, the fact that he was felicitated by the President, his different positions in several wars – everything, he knows literally everything by heart.

But the reporter also knows this information already. What's the point in noting down these details? He feels like interrupting him and saying, 'Even I know these details', but doesn't break his flow of thought. Whatever he is letting out, the reporter notes down in his book. At least the student is finally talking and this might help him getting some essential information.

By now the reporter gets the feeling that the true essence of his interview is evading him.

The student stops as if he has got exhausted – even the reporter's pen stops.

Now what to do – stare at the student's neat and clean hostel room or stare at the walls, or look out of the window?

In the small patch of sky visible from the window, he could see a line of smoke being emitted from the chimney in the next compound.

How tiresome this interview has been! He hasn't got any worthwhile information from the student... memories... events in the family...details of his father's nature...absolutely nothing. What kind of a son is he?...Can't even relate a few details about his father!

'In which year are you studying at the moment?'

'B.E. Final.'

'Which stream?'

'Telecommunications.'

'Oh that's good. What are you planning to do next?

'I might go to America for further studies.'

'From where have you done your schooling?'

'Initially in Shimla and later I was shifted to Panchgani to a convent school. Due to dad's transfers, right from the beginning I've stayed only in hostels.'

'Right from the beginning means...?'

'Right from grade IV.'

'Oh! That means for nearly 13–14 years you have been away from home?'

'I used to go back home just for my vacations.'

Again a long pause. 'Any particular hobbies...?'

'Nothing special. But fond of reading both fiction and non-fiction.'

By now the line of smoke outside the window becomes faint.

'What are your father's hobbies?'

'He is interested in gardening. That's where he spends most of his spare time.'

'Have you ever helped him in his gardening?'

'No. I didn't get a chance to do so. Most of the time I've been at my hostel.'

By now, the reporter was losing his patience. No further questions were coming to his mind.

'Would you like to add anything else?'

'Um…Nothing special.'

'Any memories or events to be narrated?'

'Memories…' Goes into a trance. Looks at the ceiling, and the reporter looks at him impatiently.

'I really don't remember anything specific about dad. He used to spend his spare time gardening and was also interested in travelling.'

Oh my god! What kind of a son is this? His dad has become the Commander-in-Chief of the Indian Army, and the son…!

The reporter is about to end the interview.

'Okay then. Would you like to tell me anything else?'

'No. Right now I can't remember anything. But when I remember I will…' The voice is choked – like that of a school child who is feeling guilty for not failing to given an answer. 'If I remember, I will definitely let you know. Can you give me your contact number?'

I have really wasted my precious time with this student – he doesn't remember a single damn thing! What is he going to tell me later?

The reporter gives him the contact number.

'Shall I take your leave?'

'Hmm…Yes…'

'One more thing…Do you have any photographs?'

'No. I don't have any over here. They are at home.'

'It's okay.'

'I am extremely sorry. Was unable to provide you with too many details.'

'No, no, it's okay. If you do remember anything, just give me a call.'

'Definitely.'

While looking at him, the reporter stuffs his pen and notebook into his pocket. Shakes hands with the student and goes out.

The student closes the door of his room. Opens the morning newspaper to read the news again. Looks out of the window restlessly. Looks at the empty chair…The reporter's annoyed and helpless face hovers in his mind.

What could I do? He wonders.

In spite of telling the reporter several times that I did not remember anything, there was clear disbelief on his face. I spent most of my time in the hostels and whenever I came home for the holidays, dad would hardly be around for five-ten days, being mostly on tours. Obviously I had absolutely nothing to talk about.

Locks the room and leaves for the post office. Takes a form to write a telegram and scribbles a note.

'Dear Dad. Congratulations.'

The telegram clerk, before counting the words, reads the message, looks at the student and then back again at the telegram. Looks as if he has remembered something and with a familiar smile on his face, bends down to write something.

Without counting the change he has received, the student puts it in his pocket and starts walking towards the hostel. Because if he gets late, he will miss the hot water for his bath...

The Bridge

THE OVERHEAD FAN WAS whirling with intermittent groans. She couldn't hear what her mom was saying over the noise. Keeping aside the mobile phone that was stuck to her ears, she screamed aloud, 'What?'

Her mother was startled. 'Why are you screaming? Speak softly. It has become just impossible to talk with you,' she said. Wiping the sweat on the forehead, her mother muttered something more which was not at all audible to her.

She didn't want to talk as she thought it would be the usual rhetorical conversation. She again stuck the earbuds of her phone on. But the call soon ended or was brought to an end. 'Whenever I am talking something important over the phone, these people need to grit!' she said and banged the mobile phone on the bed. The fan continued to whirl with groans, cricks and a distinct purring.

'How many times I have told you, "Change the fan, change the fan" but no one listens! Is it necessary to keep repairing the fan till it gives out? And what do you mean that we should not "dispose of it in working condition"? Is this fan working?'

The father did not say anything. He has stopped arguing with her nowadays. Every day she starts an argument on some silly matter. An earning, unmarried daughter is difficult to handle. She has come to know that he overlooks most of the domestic matters. At the same time, he didn't want her to personally look into those matters and get them sorted out.

Muttering 'shit' to herself, she got up. She wanted to sleep for some more time. With that early morning phone call and the hassle with her mom, she lost her mood of going back to sleep.

There is only one holiday in the entire week and what a start! She pulled out the ear-phones. Throwing the hair clip on the table, she loosened her hair open. Taking some clothes, she went to bathe. On her way to the bathroom, she realized that her father, who was sitting in the room outside, was viewing her movements attentively through the passage.

Knowing that she won't be coming out for at least half an hour, her mother took out vegetables from the fridge. She knew her daughter did not like any of the vegetables she had and she pondered which vegetable to cook for her.

Her father had already taken his bath. He now wore a shirt and slid his feet into his sandals. Saying 'Will be back soon,' he pushed the door and left. Her mother didn't say a word. A single nod or a word is enough to start a fight so she thought it was better to cut vegetables than to respond to the innocuous remark by her husband. She pulled the capsicum in front of her, washed it, wiped it dry, took the sharp but heavy knife which her daughter had bought for her and sat down to cut the vegetable.

While giving her mom the knife, she had told her, 'Be very careful while cutting; it's very sharp. Else you will cut your finger.'

'Her tongue also has become very sharp like the knife. From where has she learnt to shout at us?' The mother thought while dicing the large green capsicum.

'She wasn't like this earlier,' said the mother.

'Then how was she? Meek and docile like you?'

'No, no. Not like that. But earlier she never used to grit over every word.'

'Then she had not sprouted her horns. Now that she has taken up a job, earning double her father's salary, her ego is swollen.'

'You keep harping on her salary. Obviously, she gets irritated.'

'When do I harp on her salary? I just told her not to change the fan. You know what she said? – "You don't worry about the money. I will get it while coming in the evening."'

'But what's wrong if she gets it?'

'Let her get it. When did I say no? I do not have any problem. She has too much money. She thinks anything can be bought with it. Forget about us. This is the case everywhere. Why should one listen?'

'It's okay. Let it be.'

'What do you mean by – it's okay…let it be? If this is her attitude, who will marry her?'

This is the way the parents' conversation went in her absence.

THE MOTHER CUT the vegetables and poured oil into the hot wok. Reaching across the stove, she opened the window. The overflowing garbage in the back lane was not visible but the strong stench immediately entered the house. She tempered some spices in the oil, added the cut vegetables, gave the whole thing a good stir and then seasoned by sprinkling powdered garam masala. As soon as she finished seasoning, she again closed the window because she knew that her daughter will be back from her bath any time and would not approve of the open window.

By the time she was kneading the dough, her daughter had finished bathing. 'There's absolutely no use of this girl. On other days she is busy, but at least on a holiday she should lend a helping hand. What he says is right to some extent. I have pampered her too much. I really wonder how she's going to survive later. Why should I worry? She will surely get someone with a thick, fat salary. She will be able to afford two-three maids to look after her. Why will she have to enter the kitchen?' Consoling herself, she dabbed the last tap on the dough and covered it.

After coming out of the bathroom, the daughter rubbed her hair dry. She was still feeling sleepy. The mother pulled the wooden board and rolling pin for rolling out the chapattis, the flat breads that puffed up when roasted over a flame. A strong, flowery smell spread over the house. 'She has sprayed her expensive scent. It means she is going to dress up and go out somewhere.' Her hands stopped. 'For whom should I roll the chapattis? As it is, she doesn't eat anything at home. Why doesn't she like what I cook these days? How come within merely two years her tastebuds changed so radically?'

'How much perfume do you pour on your body?' She shouted at her once, long back.

'Oh mom! This is not perfume. It's called deo.'

'That only. Whatever it is called. But how strong that smell is! Please apply mildly.'

'Oh no! You know, I travel by a crowded local train, work for the whole day and perspire a lot. I sit in an air-conditioned room; so I require it.'

After that she never broached the topic but she felt certain that this strong, reeking scent must be penetrating every pore of the building. Everybody knew who is going out with her strong 'deo smell'. She was sure no one else used as much perfume or deo as her daughter.

'I'm going out. Don't wait for me at lunch…'

Before her mother could say anything, she was already out

of the house. Her mother only hoped that she did not cross her father on the staircase. Seeing her deep-necked blouse, he would get wild and then the entire day will go in blabbering about it. She kept aside half of the kneaded dough in a small bowl.

She had got accustomed to her daughter being out until evening. She knew that when she returned, she will say that her tummy was full. Thus, she won't have her dinner too.

There was nothing to see on TV. She unnecessarily changed some two-three channels before switching it off. Pacing up and down, she called Surve, the next-door neighbour. Her husband had not come back home. 'Where has he gone? He must be hungry. He did not even have his breakfast.'

The door was open. She didn't notice him coming inside. He went to the bathroom to wash his hands and feet. When she heard the sound of water from the tap, she knew he was home. He hung his shirt on a hanger and sat on a chair near the small dining table at the corner which could accommodate only two persons. He did not ask about his daughter.

Without saying a word, she kept bowls and a plate in front of him and served him lentils, vegetable, salad, chapatti and curd. On Sundays, he would remove his shirt and sit for lunch. On other days, he is in such a hurry to go back to his work that he would eat dressed up.

'What happened? Why were you late?' she asked to break the ice, unable to bear the silence.

He didn't seem to hear her. He was probably annoyed

with his daughter for going out on a holiday and not having lunch at home. But he didn't say anything. By now she knew when best to leave things alone.

After a while he said, 'Patkar is not well. While returning, I visited him. He was discharged from the hospital. Gosh! The amount he was billed! Just don't ask.'

'Was he there for many days?'

'Yes, almost fifteen days. It seems the daily charges were two thousand rupees. Moreover, he had to spend a lot on medication, injections and other stuff.'

Both of them finished their lunch and got up to wash their hands. As usual, she cleaned the kitchen counters and kept all the leftovers in the fridge. She had rolled only five chapattis, but one-half was left untouched. The kneaded dough was ready too. If her daughter returned and wanted to eat, she would roll some more.

By the time she could finish off her daily after-meal chores and come out, he was already seated on the sofa. It couldn't be predicted when he would lie down. He had the remote in his hand but had not switched on the TV. He picked up the newspaper and flipped through its pages. The LCD TV stood out among the junk that was kept as storage.

Long back, during a heated argument, he had blurted out, 'In my unkempt house, both your daughter and this LCD TV don't fit in.'

She folded her daughter's clothes which she had left on the bed and kept them in the rack. She entered her room and was about to lie down on the bed when she remembered something. Going into the kitchen, she opened a small tin which was kept in the corner, took a pinch of mouth freshener and put it into her mouth. She then pulled two pillows off the bed and lied down on the floor.

Watching the wavering reflections of TV visuals on the half-open, laminated door, she did not know when her eyes closed and she drifted off to sleep.

In the living room, although the TV was on, he was looking into infinity beyond the moving pictures. He couldn't remember when he fell into this strange habit. His daughter's untimely shift duties and irregular sleep routines...If the TV was on, her sleep got disturbed. That was why he started watching TV without the sound. Now he was used to watching mute moving images – afternoon news, movie songs, serials – intermittently changing channels. 'Sound or no sound, Hindi channel or some other channel...What difference does it make? What's wrong with watching it without sound? One can understand a lot even by seeing these moving images.' Whether she is there at home or not – in the afternoon or at late night, he has got habituated to switching on the TV without its sound.

His wife was sleeping. Only the groans and moans of the overhead fan were audible. The silence was broken now and then by the sound of a rickshaw bell, a car or a bus crossing by, honking or the ear-corroding screeching of brakes. Once in a while, he would hear the faint voices of people walking on the road below.

He removed his vest and moved his hand over his tummy.

It was just impossible to get rid of the layers and layers of sweat on his neck. The buildings have been constructed so close to each other that there is no scope for even a little breeze to flow in. The fan makes only noise, doesn't stir the air. On TV, Mickey Mouse and Goofy were up to something. He switched to another channel which was showing a wildlife safari.

Watching this, he lay down. The TV remained on as he nodded off despite his resolve to switch it off before sleeping.

As soon as he drifted into sleep, he started getting an illusion that he was walking over the Thane Creek's bridge, carrying a trunk in his hand. His wife was walking behind him with a flour container on her waist followed by his daughter with a mobile phone in her hand. They were walking across it for quite a long period of time.

As SOON AS SHE GOT OFF the bridge, she got a rickshaw. That was lucky as getting a rickshaw has become a very difficult task. Although the distance was walkable, she didn't like to walk. She thought that everyone intently stared at her. Her father always walked. He justified it by saying 'it's for the exercise' and she got irritated. She did not know that the bitter truth is that he saved Rs 20 every day and, ultimately, Rs 400 is saved in a month. Since it was a Sunday, most of the commuters were with their families, yet it was not crowded in the First Class compartment. She got a window seat easily. When the train started, she felt better because of the breeze. She didn't know the reason but she experienced a sense of freedom when she used to cross the Thane Creek's bridge. She used to feel as if she had entered into an altogether different world. Actually, she would have loved to stay somewhere on the other side of the creek near Mumbai city but her parents wouldn't like the idea of shifting as it is not practical.

The mother was tossing and turning. She didn't know when she drifted into sleep. It was not sleep but languor. She was thinking about her daughter. In her dream, she was wearing good clothes suitable for a festive occasion and waiting for her daughter. He was, as usual, invisible. It was pitch black. It was not cloudy but very dark. The darkness was fearsome. How come she has not returned? She had promised that she will be back early. Perhaps she had some meeting in the office.

No one escapes from the clutches – right from a housemaid to a corporate lady boss. The daily newspapers are full of all kinds of ominous news – rape, murder, kidnapping and what not. The same news is heard on the news channels throughout the twenty-four hours. In TV serials, it's the same. She gets petrified seeing and hearing similar content all the time.

The crowd isn't lessening. If a new local arrives, it becomes more crowded. Raising herself, the mother tries to look out for her. Unexpectedly, she is seen right in front of her. Two-three people are holding her and helping her to move ahead. Her daughter is crying and while wiping her face, she is trying to hide her face. Her clothes are soiled and muddy. Scratches are seen on her hands. She starts crying bitterly, but there isn't any kind of noise coming out from her throat.

At that moment, she woke up with a start. She realized that she was sweating profusely. She wiped her sweat with the pallu of her sari. Muttering to herself 'Oh gosh! What a dream!' she came out.

He was lying asleep on the sofa. The TV was on and a familiar, rhythmic, snoring sound was audible. Ignoring his snores, she went to the kitchen and drank a glassful of water.

When the doorbell rang, he came out of his trance. Putting on his vest, he went to open the door. She was at the door with a weary face.

Ignoring the question mark on both of their faces, she entered the house and went straight to her room. Without even changing her clothes, she threw herself on the bed. She slept till 9 p.m. – time for dinner.

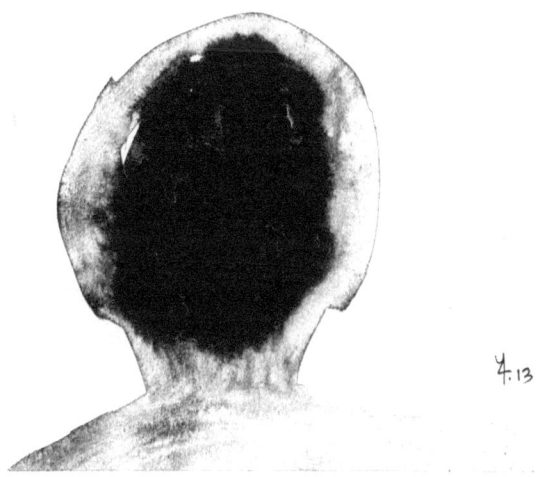

4.13

Deshmukh

WHEN I GENTLY SLID ASIDE an old tattered file, he caught my attention. He was watching me intently. There is hardly any visitor for me in office. Even when there are, they are either relatives or old school and college friends.

For the four-five tables in the room, there is only one metal chair for visitors. Whoever comes positions the chair facing the person to meet. Even without lifting one's head, one comes to know whom the visitor has come to meet. It's because of the screeching sound the chair makes when being pulled. This gentleman had moved the chair to sit in such a position that it was impossible to guess whom he had come to meet. He seemed to have been sitting for quite some time.

The chair hadn't made any noise either. No one had lifted their head. Some were reading books, hiding them in the files, one was crunching numbers of monthly accounts, another was looking blankly into a file and scrawling lines on a paper. The woman sitting across me had pulled back her chair, lifted up her legs and rested her knees against the edge of the table. She was sitting in such a position that no one would realize that she was knitting. The wool yarn came up softly at intervals from below her table. That means no one had realized that this gentleman had come.

Without making any noise, he had quietly pulled the chair to the present position. I was surprised because these days hardly anyone cares for others. Whoever comes, pulls the chair to sit and never bothers to care about others sitting around busy with their own work or simply dozing off.

Even if the chair had made some noise, it wouldn't have affected anyone. Everybody was used to its screeching sound. Only while exiting the boss's cabin, everyone took precaution of closing the door gently behind them. If one left in a hurry, the door would bang and produce a loud noise, offending the boss. Obviously, all eyes would turn towards the cabin. Sometimes he got very annoyed and called the person back and yelled, 'Don't you know how to close the door quietly?' When he got angry, his voice was louder than the banging of the door.

Thousands of sounds keep mixing with plenty of words, forever flowing in this office. If this person had been working in our company, then he would have definitely been in the good books of our boss and probably would have managed to even get two-three promotions. The boss wouldn't have noticed this person's entry and exit. His files would have been easily cleared by the boss without any fuss.

He was sitting right in front. Not a single muscle on his face made any movement. What the hell? Why was he staring at me?

One thing was for sure, he must be definitely in awe of the person whom he has come to meet. Otherwise he wouldn't have sat so quietly, drawing the chair silently and waiting to seek that person's attention.

I jerked my head. The crackling sound of bones was heard across the room. I shook off laziness to free myself of boredom.

'Yes. What can I do for you? Whom do you want to meet?' I asked since he had moved a bit closer. His hands were now on my table.

'If I'm not mistaken – are you Mr Vinayak?'

'Yes.'

My eyes shimmered with questions, but his gave a cold look. Since he had asked the first question, it was natural for me to expect that he should have introduced himself. But he was quiet. I was wondering – who he is, from where, for what and why has he come?

The hands that were kept on the table looked quite fair. The long and straight fingers with bluish, bulging, conspicuous veins indicated that he was quite mature. His untrimmed beard also gave the same impression. He was wearing a clean, pure white shirt and 'Killer' jeans, with a blue canvas bag hung on the shoulder. I was unable to guess much about him.

He had a subservient look on his face with calm, composed and shining eyes. Actually I'm not into the habit of staring at anyone. I even avoid eye contact. But his eyes had the sharp edge of a surgeon's weapon that made me uneasy.

'Do you recognize me?'

An unexpected question put with a lot of self-confidence. Generally, there is a way of introducing oneself. Such mystifying, daring questions bordering on insolence indicated the questioner's cool disposition.

'Um…I have seen you somewhere…' I muttered as I looked down at his brand new Kolhapuri chappals, with the tassel looking still new.

'Absolutely wrong. You're seeing me for the first time. That means we are absolute strangers. Right?'

I was stumped. Even if we hadn't met anytime earlier, at least for the sake of etiquette, when I said that I had seen him somewhere, he could have said something like – 'Yes, might be possible' or 'there are many people who look alike' and could have come to the point. But he didn't do so. Why did he retort so arrogantly? It was merely for the sake of a formality that I had said, 'I have seen you somewhere.'

The notion that I had formed about him – especially when he sat without making a noise, the politeness in the body language, his calm and sober facial expressions – was completely shattered the minute he opened his mouth. I was not only angry with that single sentence of his, but firmly believed that he must be a self-opinionated man.

As it is I don't like personal visitors in my office. Not even my close friends, except when there is an emergency or some urgent work. This arrogant stranger – I felt like cutting him short and avoiding him. However, I became curious about him.

The fan was noisily rotating, barely ruffling the air in the room. I removed my folded handkerchief, wiped the sweat off my forehead, inclined back a bit in the chair and looked around. He didn't expect an answer for his question. I became quite uneasy when I realized that he was looking intently at my fingers. I again looked around. No one was looking at him or even at me. His voice was very soft and had a hint of crudeness.

There was a familiar flow of noise. Every day's useless hustle and bustle, handover of files, clacking of boots and chappals.

Putting back the folded handkerchief into my pocket, I leaned forward.

'Yes? Tell me.'

He didn't take any heed of what I said and his eyes were now fixed on my stomach. As if he wanted to cut through it and see what was there inside. What else will there be? Two chapattis, okra stir fry, peanut chutney and batatawada (the local spicy potato burger) ordered from the office canteen. These days, chapattis are quite singed. Perhaps he saw that too? Although I did not say a thing, I became quite uneasy.

Who was he and from where had he come? He too was silent. When he had spoken, his speech was very fast. His stare seemed to be piercingly direct. My apprehension was increasing. From my stomach, his stare now moved to the edge of the table. What did he want?

He met my glance and smiled. Unwillingly, unknowingly even I smiled but got annoyed at my own self. Why did I smile? Whatever it is, I felt this would make him talk.

'What happened?'

'What?'

'You smiled.'

So what? Was he cross-examining me? He was the one who smiled first and he was asking me why I smiled! Height of arrogance. Anyway I thought it was a good topic and smiled inwardly.

'You smiled?'

Again the same question. I was baffled. Did he know that I had smiled in my head? Of course not! He was probably repeating his first question. Without any acquaintance with me, he is hounding me with the same questions. My patience was nearing its end.

'Yes. How can I help you? Actually we don't know each other.' My voice must have clearly indicated my anger and hesitation. The volume of my voice went up a bit. I could sense that the reel of wool had taken a pause. The lady had a bad habit of eavesdropping. She was always curious to know who's who, who was saying what. I mean she was the only person in the entire staff who had all the minute details – that is, knew about the affairs – of each and every person.

The man sitting opposite me remained silent. He pulled his bag in front of him, unzipped it, peeped inside, removed a bundle of papers and kept it on the table. He took out a folded magazine from that bundle, kept it aside and put back all the remaining papers inside. The bag looked expensive.

'I suppose this is your story!'

I was taken aback, unable to comprehend anything. He unfolded that magazine and put it in front of me. That rang a bell. He was talking about the story from the magazine *Gunijan* (noblemen), which I had written two years ago. Nervously I looked around. None apart from the knitting lady was paying any attention. By now, her ears were stuck to what was going on at my desk. No one in the office knew that I write. I had made no efforts to tell anyone about it.

Gunijan was an old magazine but very few people know about it. This Hindi magazine was published from Banaras. It had articles, poems and features; volumes of poetry related to religion, spirituality and culture. Many preferred reading its summaries. It also published stories on mythology and religion. The story of Mahabharata was being serialized for fifteen years.

It would have stunned people from my office if they came to know that I was into such type of writing. They would have neither understood nor realized its importance. Initially everyone would have praised me but later I would have become an object of ridicule. This very thought made me half-dead.

By the way, I'm not a writer as such. My Hindi too is not very good. But since I read a little bit, I can write. This might be a result of listening to kirtans (religious songs) and pravachans (spiritual discourses) when I was very young. One day, I came across this magazine on a railway bookstall and bought it. I not only liked it, I became addicted to it. Soon after that, one day, I wrote a letter to the editor, which got published. I wrote another one. Then a few more. All were published. But there was one which turned out to be quite a sizeable one. I didn't see it and gave up hope but after two-three months, it was published independently in the form of an article. And this went on.

I never thought much about that. At home also, no one thought I was doing anything great. I used to receive some twenty or twenty-five rupees as a money order, which were high moments for me alone. Close friends did not show any excitement. Obviously, there was no point in telling about it to the office colleagues.

I can't say exactly what I write. I just write on current affairs with some examples in simple words. Magazines related to literature do publish stories. If my stories had got published in any literary magazine, then definitely I would have told others with pride. Frankly speaking, I did make some attempts to send my short stories to popular magazines for publication but they were turned down in quick succession. So I gave up hope.

He was holding that copy of *Gunijan* and was asking me whether I had written in it or not. I almost snatched the magazine that looked quite dated. It was the 'Warkaryachi Aai' story (The Pilgrim's Mother). What was the big deal about it? That magazine, that story, that stranger…I wasn't mentally prepared to talk about it in the office. But the way he was sitting indicated he definitely wanted to talk at length. I glanced at the clock on the opposite wall. There was ample time for us to go out for a cup of tea and be back before office got over.

I pushed the chair back, got up and stood at once.

'We have liked your story. It's excellent!'

I wasn't attentive towards what he was saying. I could see the lady had stopped knitting and was analysing everything. She is very good at that. I don't know why, but I just hate her being nosey in everyone's affairs. Why does she behave so?

'Let's go out somewhere,' I muttered, ignoring what he was saying. He also got up and followed me. I didn't realize it while he was sitting but when he stood up I noticed that he was quite a tall robust person with strong but drooping shoulders. Apart from the bright shining eyes, everything else seemed clumsy. That blue leather bag dangling from the shoulders defied the impression of poverty suggested by his crumpled soiled clothes. Instead of that fashionable bag, if he had a simple one and instead of jeans if he had worn a soiled pant or a pair of simple cotton pyjamas then it would have given the impression of a young unemployed person wandering in search of a job. And even the boldness in the eyes would have seemed like helplessness and dejection.

I was relieved to get up and leave the office. I was getting

141

irritated with his stare. I also felt a bit happy after seeing that magazine. At least I have come across someone who has read what I have been writing. But I was at my wit's end. What was he going to say? He had said that 'we' have liked the story. Who were those 'we'?

To go out of the room, I have to pass through the gap between that lady's table and mine. There is hardly any distance between our tables and I needed to be careful of the corner edge. While doing so, my hand obviously takes the support of her table to make sure that I won't be hurting myself. That day, the moment I kept my hand on the table she looked up and cast a furtive smile at me from the corner of her lips, with an 'I know why you are going out' sort of expression. I ignored her as if I hadn't noticed.

'You know we won't be able to speak comfortably in the office.' I told him while moving out. He nodded as if he has understood what I had to say. While going down the stairs there was so much commotion that it was impossible for us to talk.

By then I started to feel a bit excited. Why had he liked that story 'Warkaryachi Aai'? What was special about it? Nothing! In Hindi literature, so many saints have written on Lord Vitthal of Pandharpur. In this story, I'd tried to portray that Lord Vitthal himself is the warkari's or the pilgrim's mother or that his mother is his lord. It's an incident that had taken place with a warkari and I had described how he leaves his village and goes to stay in a monastery, how he gets engrossed in the kirtans. Unexpectedly his mother turns up there and she requests him to come home along with her. He refuses and continues to sit there. She then insists she will stay at the monastery which he refuses as well. She cries and stays there only for two days. She threatens to commit suicide at the feet of Lord Vitthal and leaves on the journey for Pandharpur. Ultimately he also does the same and neither of them return.

Of course I had written in a manner that it would show some familiarity but the incident was a fictitious one. It hadn't appealed much to me. I had sent the story and it got printed. That's all! That someone had liked it and wanted to say something about it was a pleasant surprise for me. Lord Vitthal's grace! What else?

Earlier, I was fond of listening to the kirtans and sermons, but now I am not. Long back, there used to be some programme or the other taking place at my village. My uncle used to go and I would accompany him. I didn't understand anything but loved hearing the loud acclamation of the lord by the lead singer, who sang the devotional songs with the help of musical instruments like the cymbals and the mridunga and watching him engrossed in dancing to his own tune.

On the outskirts of the village, on the banks of the river, there was a monastery of a saintly person. Many learned men, religious preceptors and masters, used to visit him. There used to be discussions on various topics. He was succeeded by his heir, a very handsome young ascetic. Day in and day out he was absorbed in reading religious scriptures. I was taken to hear his discourses when I was a child. I never understood a word of what he said but would always wonder about what his mother must be feeling…From which village he hailed. There was always a curiosity. 'Warkaryachi Aai' was thus an outcome of this. Otherwise I usually write whatever I have heard or read.

I remember an incident but haven't written about it. During the month of kartik, the eighth month of the Hindu calendar, there used to be kakad or obeisance with lighted wicks accompanied by devotional songs, aarti and bhajans, at the crack of dawn in temples of Lord Rama. There was a sort of excitement – getting up early in the morning, taking a bath and rushing to attend the ascetic's discourses in his melodious voice. One day when we reached the temple, we saw that he was holding the tambourine and others were standing quietly. Those who were sitting looked quite uneasy. His eyes were red. What must have happened? I dared to ask my uncle. He said, 'Oh dear, he reads a lot, almost until blood gets saturated in his eyes.' I just couldn't believe this but my awe and respect for him increased. Actually, everyone was waiting for the percussionist to arrive. The ascetic was a short-tempered person who didn't approve of any kind of delay in any work. He was looking very furious.

When someone cried out, 'He has come', everyone glanced towards the door. Keeping down the tambourine, trampling the people who were sitting, the ascetic rushed towards the drummer like an arrow. But the percussionist bent to bow down to him in obeisance. Ignoring his attitude, the ascetic assaulted him by giving a tight slap on his face. The percussionist remained prostrated at his feet. This mellowed down his smoldering eyes. He lifted him up lovingly holding his shoulders and loudly proclaimed the name of Lord Vitthal. Everyone joined in and everything started in a normal way as if nothing had happened. The drummer also did not fall short of any expectations. While he was rushing towards the percussionist like an arrow, the ascetic trampled on my thigh, which made me writhe in pain. That thigh pained for days together. When I had written the story, this ascetic kirtankar was somewhere at the back of my mind. For years, I hadn't visited that place. I heard he doesn't reside there and obviously the monastery has lost its glory.

After coming out of the office, I asked the visitor whether he would like to go to the Irani's hotel round the corner. Again he didn't speak a word but followed me.

I ordered for two teas and turned to him. Even if we sat there for a long time, there wouldn't be any problem, but I was not at all interested in doing so. I only wanted to know who this person was and what he wanted.

'Yes. How can I help you? You haven't introduced yourself.'

'I'm Sandipan,' he answered in a disinterested manner. Is this the way to introduce oneself? I didn't ask him anything further questions. If he isn't interested why should I ask him anything?

'I want to talk to you about what you've written. Whatever you've written is good. Written with honesty. One doesn't find such straight forward and simple writing these days.

Whatever is told, it is usually with twists and turns. But whatever you write, though may be good, is based on wrong principles, according to some of us. We want to convey to you how it is wrong, so that the next time you write, we are fully assured that you won't be repeating the mistake.'

Every sentence of his was making me feel as if I was reading an editorial. 'Ours is a group. We have discussions on such topics. We meet once a week.'

'What's the name of your group?'

'We don't have any name. Everything's informal. But most of our views do match. We have some firm notions and always make efforts to convince people. But we don't publicise it. If people get convinced, they start following what we say and, without being told, start promoting these values.

'Let me make one thing clear. We're not at all associated with any political party, social movement or established organizations. Most of the time, people misunderstand us. It will take a long time to turn our efforts into a revolution because it takes time for new trends or views to get absorbed.'

The waiter banged two cups of tea in front of us. I was listening to him and getting intrigued. I really get surprised when people express their opinion so categorically.

'Now if you ask me what's our exact job and what are our expectations, then it's difficult to explain. For that you will have to spare a lot of time for us. If our views are cogent and stand to reason then you join us, otherwise you are free to go your way. It's okay. That's the next step. And I don't worry about it.

146

'But you must come once. Every Saturday evening we meet each other. About ten of us. At times there is an outsider also. The environment is such that the outsider also gets involved in our discussion. The venue is fixed, it's secluded and there is absolute privacy. There is complete independence. We don't believe in anything illegal. There are three lady members. Even they come from faraway places. Nothing is decided. Spontaneity is our prime characteristic.'

I looked at my watch. He must have noticed it. 'I won't take much of your time but with reference to your story, some points are quite clear. The concept of a Mother and Lord are woven together. You have glorified the fact that the Lord is in fact the Mother. It's not your fault. It is the way you have been nurtured. Our fight is against such basic faiths and doctrines. These are the concepts which have proved detrimental to the progress of the entire humanity. The process of evolution has come to a standstill, since people have got entangled in the whirlpool of such doctrines. We believe that such doctrines need to be exposed thoroughly and eradicated completely.'

I looked at him. By now, everything was going over my head. I'm not in the habit of listening to such a heavy dose of verbiage. I thought he was unnecessarily wasting his time and mine. In spite of telling me that the story was good, why was he babbling like an insane person?

Looking at him, I could sense that he was talking with an ardent fervour. Being excessively affectionate or having immense love for anything is also a type of madness. The initial shine in his eyes started giving a look of insanity.

'It's okay,' he said while keeping his cup down. 'We had a discussion on your story for over three full days. Dina had brought her mother. You'll be wondering why we read a magazine like *Gunijan*. The reason is that the readers of this magazine are very innocent, they are huge in number, and are spread far and wide. So we need to take cognizance of it.

'There's a person named Firoze, who works for the betterment of small children in the age-group of three to six years. This is the age when our imagination and creativity is in full bloom. But we have kept it stagnated and loaded it with heavy rituals and doctrines. So what I'm saying is that this Firoze has sent a message for you. He has also read your story. According to him, it's based on completely wrong principles. He is ready to prove it. For that you will have to come to us and get convinced.'

This matter was taking quite a weird turn and I just could not digest it. I wasn't mentally prepared to go anywhere with him or attend any of his group meetings. At the same time, I was quite curious to know who these people were, what they did. The way he kept on talking about the entire matter, I developed a fear of unknown.

I cut him off and asked him, 'Where does your mother stay?'

There wasn't any reason for me to ask such an irrelevant personal question, that too, out of the blue. We both were startled. His flow of the speech got halted. Getting into a fix whether or not to answer, he kept on staring at me. The displeasure on his face was clearly visible.

My question seemed to hurl him down from a height. I could see the agony on his face. But the very next moment he tried to compose himself.

'Good that you have asked. These days she is in an old-age home. But it has nothing to do with our discussion. Since you asked, I am telling you.'

After that, he went on talking nonstop for over ten-fifteen minutes. But there was an uneasiness and rapidity, as if he just wanted to finish off what he had to say. Earlier, he had been speaking at an easy pace, stressing on every sentence about all his moves and was also eager to see its impact on me. But now it was as if he was blurting out something memorized.

'Feroze wants you to go along with him to the orphanage at Wadala. He works there on holidays. He meets the girls and boys over there. If you want, some of us can accompany you. He just wants you to speak with those children. Talk to them, listen to what they require, ask them questions. We will help you to understand a child's psychology. There's no urgency of going there. First you visit our place. Need not feel awkward.'

'We don't assemble there only for serious discussions. We play carrom, chess, cards. There is ample to eat. You can enjoy yourself. But these are just fringe activities. Don't think we are running a social club.

'You must go to Wadala. You meet the children and hear what they say. After reading Wordsworth and Sane Guruji, our minds have gone astray. Try to understand what notions the children have about a "mother" and then write.'

By then I had lost my cool. What the hell! Why all this trouble chasing me? I was not at all in the mood to listen to him.

'I am sorry. It's only me who has been talking. Will you come? I don't think there's any problem in visiting. I am sure you will come. You need not tell me just now. Take your time. If you want I can come again.'

'You are probably right. But I am not at all a big writer and I am not used to any kind of discussions, symposiums or intellectual consultations. Do one thing, you give me your address. I will let you know. Why unnecessarily have a fruitless trip?'

'Why call it a fruitless trip? It's my duty. And I am going to do it. If you want the address, I will give it. Come at your own leisure but let me know when we should go to Wadala. At the maximum, it will require two to three hours.'

'Okay, I will let you know,' I said and got up. He also followed me. I paid the bill. Saying 'Okay do come,' he vanished into the rush.

Assuring myself that everything was over, I kept that paper with the address in my pocket and started walking towards the office. My head had started tingling, the entire conversation hounding me.

I felt as if I have had a walk through a thoroughly congested road. In crowded places, we don't understand how long we have walked. You realize it only when you sit down to relax. Listening to him was no less than a mental agony. My body relaxed as I sat down on my chair again.

150

I sent the file I was working on through Sakharam to the boss and wiped the sweat off my forehead. Everything was going on in the usual way.

The usual sounds were flowing continuously – a familiar one. Every day's usual futile hustle and bustle, the exchange of files, the clacking of the boots and chappals and everyone's drowning into the dampness of the papers.

No one had realized that I had gone out. As it is no one takes any notice of anyone's coming or going. When I sat into my chair, I felt as if I had returned from some unknown land.

My attention was drawn towards the purse on the opposite table. When her purse is out it means it's time to go. That lady was the only one who noticed my going out. She had even heard our brief conversation in the office. She must have gone to freshen up.

I don't know how and why, but some five-six years ago, she had been transferred to our department. I have been interacting with her since then. I just don't like her. I don't like the way she talks or behaves. How to talk and behave is her personal matter. I don't have any right to speak about it but I don't feel what she does is correct. I have never told her so, but she has realized it and keeps a distance. With others she talks garrulously and shows her winsomeness but not in front of me.

Before opening her mouth to speak, she has a habit of looking into the eyes of the other person and smile coyly in a way that is certainly to be misunderstood. In fact, we realized very late that she never smiles at anyone but at herself. So people talk a lot of nonsense about her.

Long back, one day, she had told me, 'Mr Deshmukh, you are too simple. You shouldn't be such a simpleton.' I don't remember what was the reference for her observation. I don't even remember whether I answered her or not. But that sentence got fixed into my mind. Perhaps this was everyone's view about me. Even my family members must also be feeling the same. There's nothing wrong in whatever she had said but her tone was very brusque. And because of that, there has always remained a sort of grudge in my mind.

It was as if the purse on that opposite table was looking scornfully at me and laughing. I took out the paper on which the address had been written. In a very beautiful and clean handwriting he had noted the address of Wadala. Why should I keep this address in my pocket?

Just as the thought that I must throw the paper into the dustbin kept near my feet occurred to me, that lady appeared in front of me. She had combed her hair and tied a tight top-knot. Her sari was draped perfectly tight, she had washed her face and redone her make-up. The fresh application of lipstick made her lips look more prominent. On coming closer, when she realized that I was staring at her, she was a bit startled. As usual, she looked into my eyes and then gave a winsome smile. But this time it indicated that she really wanted to talk with me – might be curious to know what this 'Warkaryachi Aai' matter was after overhearing our conversation.

She came and sat back in her chair. The paper with the address written on it was still in my hand. 'Aren't you ready to leave? Or are you planning to do over-time?' she asked but my eyes were focused on the address. Without waiting for my answer, she slung the purse on her shoulder and got up.

'There was a guest, so am late,' I told her as she was passing through the gap of the two tables. The way she smiled intrigued me, making me wonder how much she had heard.

I dismissed the idea of tearing the paper and kept it back in my pocket. I must go and see what it's all about.

Amolik

IT IS ALMOST TWO YEARS since I had bumped into Amolik. There is a reason for remembering him today. While rummaging through my collection of books a few minutes back, a scrap of paper fell out.

As I came out of Churchgate station a couple of years ago, I had paused for a minute. Like ants, people were streaming into the subway leading to the suburban railway station. Very few like me were walking against the flow, trying to get out of the ant-hole. No point in trying to board a train during peak hours, I told myself while climbing the last step. I was contemplating on what to do when Amolik, my college friend, bumped into me. I had not seen him since I had left college. Feeling uncomfortable and embarrassed, I did not know how to respond to his greetings. After 'Hi' and 'Hello', I took him to the nearby Wayside Inn, my regular joint where I gulp a glass of beer before boarding a train after a gruelling day at the law firm, Desai and Desai.

Actually, there was never anything common between us – Amolik did not even belong to my group of close friends. Both of us used to occupy different rooms on the same floor of the college hostel and bumped into each other whenever we visited the small hostel canteen for our morning cup of tea. Actually, I never liked him. I found him too inquisitive. Whenever we were together, he always used to ask some irrelevant but personal information about my friends with whom he had no connection, irritating me no end. However, all those things were from the distant past and I was feeling quite happy to have met him as I had enough time to spare. I invited him for a drink at the bar.

There is a reason why I vividly remember our earlier discussions. I did not resent his blunt and direct manner but he often confused me and made me feel uncomfortable. Ah, now I do recollect that there was a smirk on his face when I asked him to share a bottle of beer with me. The smirk was not there when we entered the bar and got a table near the window. It was only after the initial pleasantries and sharing information about who is where and who we are in touch with, did I realize that there was a twisted smirk on his face and he knew exactly why it was there. But I did not mind it.

He was silently reminding me of the time when I had given up beer during our hostel days.

'Really those were happy days. No tension, no work…'

'And very little study', he completed the sentence as both of us erupted into laughter.

'We had no reasons to worry. Dad used to send money orders as there were no ATMs or bank money transfers.' I recalled how at the beginning of the month almost all of us used to wait for the postman to deliver money orders from our parents and how we used to celebrate MO day at the Irani restaurant with bun maska (buttered buns) and double omelette.

'You had a nice binge at Paud…'

I could not figure out what he was referring to and the lack of any reaction from me made him frown questioningly.

'You guys had gone to John Kale's village for testing a local brew – pahilidhar. Don't you remember?' He appeared to be confused over why I was not responding. How could I forget such an event which had become talk of the hostel those days? Like a flash it came back.

'Come on, you were not part of the gang.'

'Okay, I never was part of your gang. But we knew about it. Everybody talked about it for months. What exactly happened?'

I did not answer immediately.

'What happened? We had a great time. Open air, lot of booze and good food…'

'I know that. Something did happen. No one openly

talked about it but some whispers percolated down and we all wondered what happened at the Paud party.'

I could not understand what he was hinting at. I remember the Paud party but there was nothing significant about it. And what was there to hide? In fact, I had totally forgotten all about the party as the days and years passed by and I got busy with my career. Now that Amolik mentioned the incident, I started recalling it in bits and pieces. For Amolik, remembering things had become a habit. He himself would not participate in anything but would try to get his information second-hand by asking nosy and irritating questions. But once I realized that he meant no harm or ill-will, I began tolerating him.

'You were very upset after you returned from Paud. You did not talk to anyone for almost a week and kept to your room.' What was he saying? I could not recollect confining myself to my room and not talking with anyone for a week. I ransacked my memory and tried to recall some detail about the incident but drew a blank. This was quite embarrassing, not remembering anything about the Paud incident. It is surprising that Amolik remembers so much while I could not remember anything at all. Why? Something must have occurred, an incident or an event which must have induced partial amnesia.

What I distinctly remember is the fact that I stopped drinking beer after our visit to Paud and I never had a sip of the brew till I finished my college. I began drinking again after I joined the law firm and had to attend a number of social gatherings and interact with clients to gather information which was so vital for my seniors. What did occur at Paud which turned me into a teetotaller? I felt frustrated for not being able to recollect it. As I tried to remember what really had happened at the Paud party, the bitter taste of beer brought back some submerged memories. The picture was a little hazy and unclear but the feelings of bitterness and disgust seemed familiar. Was my mind playing a game of hide and seek?

'What are you talking yaar, I can't remember a fucking thing of that party. Okay, as you say I was not talking about it then, but there is no reason why I should not tell you now after so many years.'

'Well, you must have forgotten all about it. But those days your behaviour was different. When I had asked you about it while sipping a cup of hot steaming tea, you just flared up and asked me to fuck off. But Gupta had talked about it a little bit...'

'Maybe yaar, but I do not remember anything. Why should I keep it a secret or hide it from you or for that matter from anyone? It was plain and simple booze party and that's it.'

Is it possible that I have intuitively forgotten things which I was not comfortable with and did not want to tell him then and could not recollect now? Was it totally erased from my memory so that no one, not even I could recollect it – a total delete job?

'It was great fun and I never got such a kind of kick ever...'

Under the influence of strong beer and persistent grilling

by Amolik, my effort to remember our party at Paud was like diving deep into an ocean and rummaging through unknown depths to unearth a lost treasure trove. It was like trying to recollect sequences from a dream, and slowly but surely, images and details about the party started surfacing in my mind. I verbalized these images to Amolik; it was like seeing a mute film and talking about it frame by frame. Sometimes I would miss a link and struggle to get back to it again. A small sleepy village, dusty roads and rows of small houses with a main thoroughfare winding through dilapidated thatched cottages. Amber turned into deep grey and evening descended on the village as we entered the main lane and walked along. It ended at an old isolated church building with a wide open unkempt courtyard, a row of small outhouses at the back, hens strutting from one corner to another, cattle returning after grazing on the slopes of small hills located just behind the rows of these outhouses.

John entered one of the houses, said something to an old lady, and came back. As we started strolling towards the small hills behind the bushes, someone came out of the bushes, approached John and talked to him. We started following the stranger; John, I, Ashok and Ramesh in that order, and came to a spot below the foothills which was covered with gunny bags and a dimly lit kerosene lantern. We sat in a circle and, one by one, we got plastic glasses filled with some odourless sparkling liquid. Ramesh called it 'pahilidhar', the first drops of distilled alcohol prepared with naphtha and jaggery. There was no taste or odour, but it went down with a burning sensation. We just gulped it down, didn't look at it.

As the second round started, I don't know whether it became pitch black or we were imagining things – it was as if we had become weightless wonders. God knows! Time stood still; one by one we got up and started our return journey, almost blacked out.

As we started descending from the foot of the hill, we felt a fresh breeze making us lighter than a feather and we started floating in the air. Were we walking or floating? Dim lights of the village appeared distant, barren farms, the stars sparkled across a clear blue sky. I smiled to myself, so beautiful I told myself, as if I saw them for the first time, or did they look different from a village? I felt like singing; someone slipped down and tried to get up with great difficulty; I laughed out loudly but stopped when I saw some black shadows moving back and forth in the fields. I strained my eyes to see a herd of sheep with eyes glowing like diamonds. Together they formed a thick black cloud moving slowly, stars or eyes, clouds of sheep, confusing but soothing. Why was Gupta, I am sorry, Ashok...Why was Ashok pushing and prodding everybody from behind? Why was he in a hurry? Hungry with a rumbling stomach, I felt as if I was on a merry-go-round; looked back, there was no hill, no sheep, no trees, nothing except a barren, dead farm.

The church building glowed with a halo around it, dogs barked from a distance, in pin drop silence, a few shrill human voices mingled with each other and then silence followed. We sat down in the veranda. John went inside. An offensive odour of urine and cow dung mingled with the sound of bells hung around the necks of moaning cows. My stomach churned. 'Don't puke, you fool,' I told myself.

The kerosene lantern burned with flickering flames making our weird shadows dance to its tune. We had aluminum plates in hand with jowar bhakari (millet flatbreads) and hot egg curry. Ramesh kept on muttering something inaudible and suddenly shouted, 'Where are the fucking onions?' I tried to hold him back; his lips kept on moving without sound, eyes looked insane and focused on infinity. We felt better after swallowing some rice and curd. I washed my hands carefully, lay down on the veranda, closed my eyes and tried to sleep. I could hear chickens clucking from somewhere. Whose hand was this on my stomach? We slept for few hours, got up and walked back to the bus stand with a heavy head after profusely thanking John's friends who had fed us with good food.

I narrated these experiences as they came to my mind slowly. He listened excitedly but at the end was visibly upset at not hearing what he expected to hear. He was confused. As far as I was concerned, it was nice to recall suppressed memories of an evening out in an open field.

The images that remained with me was of those shining stars in the sky giving a mystic canopy to the whole experience. There was nothing that I remembered which made me feel ashamed or uncomfortable. There was nothing to hide from Amolik or anyone else.

'Ami, it was a fantastic experience. All that booze, the kick and the feeling of lightness, with all those black sheep and mystical stars. It was wonderful. The only thing I remember now is the star-lit sky over a huge farm...that is what I remember of Paud party.'

He did not say a word. He kept on gazing at his empty beer glass.

'But you see...,' he started saying something and abruptly stopped.

'What I told you was like recalling a recalcitrant dream.' Suddenly I realized that his glass was empty and he is staring into it.

'Want some more beer?'

'No. You must have forgotten something which you did not want to remember,' he insisted.

'Maybe I must have forgotten a few details but I don't think it's anything important or embarrassing or ugly.'

'Were there any girls when you had your dinner?'

'Girls?'

He remained silent, allowing me to think.

'Yes, there were two girls in the family which served us food and provided an open veranda to sleep. They were just around to help their mother when she served us food. But there was nothing peculiar to remember about them.'

'Gupta had mentioned them, that's how I knew about them. Did Ramesh make any tamasha? A spectacle?'

'Tamasha? Of course not! He was totally out.'

'Maybe he tried to molest one of the girls.'

'No. No such thing happened. What are you saying? If any

such thing had happened I'd have certainly remembered it.'

That was the end of our conversation and drinking session. I paid the bill and walked out of the bar. I do not know how much credence he gave to my reply. Once again I tried to recall the Paud experience. Almost five years had gone by but I am sure nothing of that sort had happened in Paud. I had not remembered about the two girls while I was recalling the Paud experience. Can I be categorically sure that nothing of the sort happened that night? This question troubled me.

As days passed by, that nagging question and the swirling memories of Paud got buried once again as I got busy with my own work at the law firm.

There was so much of clutter around that I rarely found what I wanted. Books, notebooks, clippings, photographs, torn pieces of paper, scribble pads. I've been meaning to clear away the mess but am always postponing the matter. Today I forced myself to rummage through old papers and books so that I could decide what to throw and what to keep. While sifting through books from my campus days, two sheets of handwritten papers attracted my attention. I had written on both sides of both the papers.

The first line startled me…

'I had no desire to go but John and Ramesh kept on persisting and forced me accompany them to Paud.' I scooped up the papers as if I had unearthed a treasure. I moved closer to the window and began reading my own handwriting.

'I had no desire to go but John and Ramesh kept on persisting and forced me accompany them to Paud. Some change in the routine. It took half an hour to reach Paud by bus. The bus station was nothing but a small shanty structure with just enough open space to allow the bus to take a U-turn. We had to cross the village before we reached an old church which stood out as the only concrete structure in the area. John's father once worked in this place and he knew a couple of families. We dumped our rucksacks at the outhouse. John told the landlady that we will be back in half an hour. She merely nodded her head.

'We began walking towards the hills and crossed two or three farms – it was difficult to walk across the uneven land. We reached a small hill which had a cluster of mango trees encircled by grey bushes. The hill overlooked a plateau which led to a barren ridge. Huffing and puffing, we reached another cluster of mango trees where a worn-out tarpaulin was hung over a small home-made distillery. There were drums of naptha and jaggery lying around haphazardly. Two persons, apart from the one who lead us to the spot, were hard at work. Wearing loose white shirts and pyjamas and rubber slippers, their unshaven faces looked fearsome but they wore reassuring smiles.

'We were among illicit liquor distillers, eager to consume pahilidhar, a country brew known for its knockout punch. We were a little relaxed as no one knew us here. We sat in a small circle near the trunk of a mango tree. John was called by our tour guide who whispered something in his ears and returned to join us. "Now guys, relax and drink to your heart. But be careful, it will give you the kick of your lifetime. Cheers."

We were given small plastic glasses of different colours. I got red while Ramesh got blue and Gupta got a yellow glass that looked dirty. Someone came with a rubber balloon filled up with liquor and poured it into our glasses. There was no colour, taste or odour. Was it some kind of elixir, a somras – a drink for the gods?

'It went down well, though there was a burning sensation when we gulped it down. Even before the first glass got emptied, I began feeling lighter. As usual, Ramesh started talking loudly but there was no need to worry since we were not disturbing anybody, nor were we sitting in any pub or restaurant.

'"Wooow, fantastic yaar, I have never tasted anything like this before. Thanks John, you are great! What an ambience, trees, bushes, blue sky and hills to give us company, cheers, boss…" He went on talking and within no time he became inaudible. I could not make out what he was saying unless I concentrated on his words. When we were served the second round, Ramesh held on to the hands of the fellow and praised him to the skies. We climbed down slowly and by the time we reached the cluster of farms, it had become pitch dark. Our guide turned back after ensuring that we had reached our destination. John tried to say something but we could not understand his words. Perhaps he wanted us to thank the fellow but we were struggling to keep our balance.

'It must have taken some time for us to reach the farm. Ramesh was giving a lecture, hectoring and talking nonstop. Gupta hurried as it was getting quite late and we could hear dogs barking somewhere. There was a herd of sheep grazing in the field which appeared ghostly as they kept on moving ahead of us. It was scary. Reaching the farm, we slumped on the veranda. An elderly person was sitting there with his grey head buried between his legs; probably the landlady's husband. He appeared to be sozzled and now waiting for food. John went inside to check for our food. "Please welcome, sir," that elderly fellow said and almost went back to sleep. Ramesh was constantly repeating himself while Gupta was restless with hunger. Both followed John into the kitchen who brought them back saying, "Just wait here for a few minutes...hot and spicy food will be ready soon."

'"Oh, let us give them a helping hand," Ramesh said and wobbled back to the kitchen where the lady and her two daughters were preparing cucumber and tomato salad. One was cutting onions and wiping away tears. Ramesh went and sat near her, grabbed a plate and volunteered to slice onions. 'Just move aside, I'll help you...,' he babbled. The girl got up and stood near a window. The woman got up and took away the plate and knife from Ramesh saying, 'Sahib, just leave it alone. You will cut your fingers.' Meanwhile, John and I tried to cajole him out of the kitchen.

'"What the hell. Do you think I am drunk? Get away. Let me help those poor girls. You idiots! You just sit here and watch. You don't want to help them because you are chauvinists..." We tried to make him sit but he preferred to stand and give a lecture on women's lib and all that. Actually, it was a good diversion as the women were left alone to cram the plates with hot steaming food – jowar bhakari, egg curry, chicken and salad with lots of onions. The food was good and tasty and we ate and ate. "Sorry auntie, we troubled you a lot," we mumbled as we enjoyed the food. "Sorry, we cannot offer you anything more delicious," she said apologetically and kept on stuffing our plates. We washed our hands and laid down on the veranda with pillows under our heads…John had magically got them from somewhere. Gupta was the first to start snoring. Meanwhile, the lady and the girls along with the grey-haired man finished off the leftovers. John went inside when someone called out to him. I was just dozing, waiting for sleep to take over, when I heard a chanting. Ramesh woke up and went inside the house.

'They were sitting in a circle around a lantern. John had a crumpled book in his hand and he was reciting something and others followed him in hushed voices with folded hands. John said, "Hey Prabhoo…O Lord!" The younger girl was a little louder than others. Ramesh sat near John and tried to peep into the book. I sat next to him, worried that he may create a scene. He sat quietly throughout the prayer till John closed the book and his eyes. Ramesh began his sermon in an unsure but loud voice, "I am happy we prayed for Yeshu, for Jesus. After all, there is only one god. We may call him with different names. As Swami Vivekanand once said: even though god is one, we have different ways to approach him…" and he went on rambling. The grey-haired man slipped out of the room and went to sleep in one corner in the veranda. I tried to stop Ramesh's slur but he now stared speaking to the landlady, "Auntie…tell me…if I am wrong…let me speak."

'Finally we pulled him out of the room. John kept Ramesh between us and we tried to sleep. My stomach was making strange noises. The stench of cattle urine and cow dung became more offensive as night descended, almost making me sick. My throat had become dry and I could hardly sleep as chickens kept shuffling their wings and disturbing the peace. The door opened, the landlady peeped out, saw everyone asleep, went inside quietly and put out the lantern. Ramesh must have tried to get up once or twice but John kept pulling him down saying, "Just sleep, man." I did manage to doze off as a cool breeze swept through the veranda. I got up with a heavy head, brushed my teeth, had a cup of tea and we soon began our return journey after profusely thanking the family.'

I finished reading the pages without a pause. I was not much disappointed with what I read but I could not figure out why I took the trouble to jot down these events on a piece of paper. I read it again. Did I have a premonition that I would forget the adventure and therefore made detailed notes? But there were no grisly details that Amolik was expecting. Yes, Ramesh did go inside and tried to snatch some onions and a knife from the girl but there was nothing outrageous about it. In fact, the incident was hilarious and perhaps slipped from my mind as time went by.

Over a glass of beer, I had narrated my impressions and memories of Paud to Amolik. It was full of brightly-lit skies with stars, sheep with diamond-like eyes, there was a recitation of poems and all that stuff which made the event very memorable. But when I read the notes, I did not find any mention of awkward impressions of Paud. What I had recalled about the trip to Amolik – did I romanticize it and talk about hills, farms, sky and sheep? Strangely, I had not remembered Ramesh's lecture, his encroachment in the kitchen, and the nauseating smells and sounds. Only common to both memories was the veranda, a mystic church building, the simple hardworking landlady and good food. It was as if my memory provided a long shot while the notes written down on a piece of paper were a closer look from a microscope.

What is reality and what is illusion? I kept on staring at the paper and tried to recall my hostel days. At the end, I was not sure whether I remembered everything, even after reading the notes. I do not now remember how the landlady looked except the way she had wrapped herself in a nine-yard sari and covered her head with its pallu. I did not look at her while leaving her house.

'Come back again, boys,' she had said. Much before her invitation, I had decided not to get involved in such parties as I was feeling uneasy with a reeling and aching head. It was like floating on thin air and then dropping down like a rock.

What ugly incident was Amolik referring to? Did it really happen or was it a figment of his imagination? I had thought it was a case of rumour mongering and nothing more. But after reading my notes, I'm quite unsure of myself. Has my mind erased unpleasant memories? There was one more fellow along with John, Ramesh and Gupta. But I have forgotten his name, nor is he mentioned in the pages that I had noted down. I don't even remember his face. John was the most sober among us. If I meet him again he may be able to throw some light.

Need to Visit

THERE WASN'T ANY NEED but it wouldn't have been proper if I did not pay a visit. I hadn't been to their place for so long that I wondered whether they would miss me if I didn't go. As my mother used to say, 'We usually visit friends and family at leisure but at such times, one must definitely pay a visit even if you are busy.'

In fact I came to know very late that his mother had expired. I had some work with him and had called. Some unknown person answered the phone and told me that he was in mourning as he had lost his mother. I didn't know what to say and spoke with hesitation, 'I'm Satish this side.

Is anyone else available?' There was no response for a while and then the person spoke up with some anger, 'His mother has expired, so you won't be able to meet him.' I wanted to ask when did this happen but before I could say anything, he had already disconnected. While he held the line, I could hear people around him talking, murmuring, and even small children crying. The person on the phone must have been talking with someone else too in the room. Whenever he would talk with that person, he probably covered the receiver with his hand and a strange silence would be created. This silence came twice my way.

I also wanted to tell him my name again because if he knew me, he would have given the phone to Tai, my cousin sister. In fact, I should have asked for Tai in the first place, but the news that her husband's mother had expired was so unexpected that it didn't strike me.

Frankly speaking, I don't have a close relationship with Tai and her family. Tai is much younger than her husband. My mom had told me that she is my second cousin. I vaguely remember that she had visited our house once when I was small. I kept touching her very soft clothes. I don't know whether I actually remember her visit or just feel that I remember because of my mother telling me about her visit. Whatever it be, she had come to our place – that was sure.

After many years, I had some work so I found out her residential address and met her. I got my job because of her husband. After I received my first salary, I had taken sweets to their place and touched their feet to get their blessings. She was very happy.

Tai is quite attached to all of us and is proud of her relatives. If I don't visit their house for some months, she would bluntly say, 'My people come only when they have work; on other days they don't even show their faces'. Basically she is brusque in her speech! Good that her husband is very understanding or else there would have been fights everyday. He might be purposely avoiding arguments knowing her nature. Sometimes she asks such weird questions that people around her get embarrassed. At such times they behave as if they have not heard her question and broach some other topic.

I feel quite awkward when I visit her home. My sister is loquacious and talks without inhibition whereas his speech is composed, measured but full of affection. She may have the habit of picking holes in everything, but she is very hospitable. Let any number of guests arrive, she will never knit her brows. No one leaves her home without lunch or dinner.

So I must visit her. Then why delay? By the time I could wind up the day's work, it had already become dark outside. I started on my way but was feeling uncomfortable. Consoling someone is actually a very difficult job. In this case, it was quite awkward. In fact, he was quite elder to me.

When I rang the doorbell, I sensed a strange quietness. At other times, there is always commotion around. Loud songs are being played on the radio or record player. Not today.

The door is opened by a servant. Like other times, he

175

doesn't smile but keeps the door open and goes inside. There is no movement and the drawing room, in spite of being completely packed, looks empty.

'Yes dear, please come in.' Tai is seated. I look around, remove my chappals and quickly sit in the nearest available chair.

'How did you come to know?'

'I had called up some time ago.'

'Oh! Is that so? Sorry dear. I didn't know that! Till some time ago everyone was here. Just few minutes ago, they left. Tatyarao…Maai…aunty…'

A middle-aged person is sitting in the chair beyond. I don't remember seeing him earlier. He might be her brother-in-law. I try to make out from the shape of his face and his complexion. On the sofa, which is behind Tai, there is a lady – might be the wife of Tai's brother-in-law. Next to the sofa was a divan on which a tiny four-year-old skinny boy is playing with a small girl who is even younger. The lady is every now and then warning them – 'Keep quiet…Are you going to keep quiet or not? Else when uncle comes, he will give you a nice pasting.' The kids pay no attention and keep playing.

Pappu, Tai's son, is studying in grade X. However, he certainly doesn't act so. This was probably due to the pampering by his parents. Even though he has grown up, they treat him like a small child. He never talks or mingles with anyone – he's reticent and curt in behaviour. He has neither Tai's loquaciousness nor his father's affectionate nature. He is lying down on the sofa, next to the TV and going through a book. When I entered, he gave me a smile – quite unlike his usual nature.

'You see, it happened so all of a sudden…'

I just listen. What should I say? That middle-aged man is scratching his ear and the lady busy quietening those children. Pappu is reading comics as if he's a total stranger to all.

'When did she expire?'

'Six days ago. I didn't get time to inform anyone. Why to trouble everyone?'

'But how come all of a sudden?'

'Yes. No one had the least idea. She didn't have any ailment. No illness, nor any complaint till the end. She had become a bit delirious, that's all.'

She used to sit on the sofa on which right now Pappu is sitting. People used to come and go. But she would be seated on that sofa. Day in and out she used to be seated there. It was her favourite place. If she felt bored, taking the support of the wall, she would go inside. No one used to pay any heed to her existence. But she didn't have any complaint regarding that. The only thing she asked for was that in the afternoon, at the tea-time, she had to have tea. If she didn't get it on time she would ask, 'Have you prepared tea or not? You haven't yet given me.' After having her tea she would again sit quietly, reclined on her sofa. If by any chance she forgot whether she had drank the tea or not, she would ask again, 'Haven't you prepared the tea?' In spite of telling her many a time that she has been given tea some time ago, she would ask for it again.

Finally if she was shown the teapot, she would keep quiet. 'Oh that means today's tea has been done!'

In spite of getting tea twice, if she felt that she had not got tea, then in the evening when Tai's husband would come, she would go to him asking, 'Sadu, have you come? Oh dear! After you leave, is there anyone who cares for me? Today no one has given me tea. At least you give me.'

'Oh Aai, you have already drank it in the afternoon and the doctor has restricted you from drinking too much of tea.'

'Where am I asking too many times? At least give once to this poor oldie!'

If Tai heard this from the kitchen she would start her wrangle, 'We go round and round for her the whole day, and this is what you get to hear at the end of the day – that I don't serve her tea!' Then she would come out and start shouting, since the old lady had a hearing problem. 'Oh my god! Haven't I given you tea in the evening? You have already drank it. See this – your cup and saucer!' She would hold an empty cup and saucer in front of her. The old lady would keep gazing at that empty cup and saucer. Without saying anything, he would either go out or into an inner room.

'She only complained there was a pain in her chest. That's all! Immediately we took her to the hospital. She has never ever complained about anything.'

'Was it a heart attack?'

'No. The doctor told some other name. She was admitted only for a day in the hospital. But it's good that fortunately she didn't suffer much.'

The commotion of the children has increased a bit. The small girl is laughing aloud while the boy is crying. The mother's attention is divided between listening to our conversation and looking after them.

She passes on an order-cum-warning to her husband, 'Will you please say something to the children? Can't you see how much they are troubling me?'

That fellow gives a startled look at her and gets up from his stupor. He bends forward and drags the girl to him. She cries out loudly. The tiny thin child stops crying and stares at me.

Tai, squatting on the floor, is right in the middle of the drawing room. In front of her is her daughter, who is in the ninth grade, sitting with open hair and bent neck. Her hair is infested with lice. Is Tai able to see in that light? She is talking with me and simultaneously combing her daughter's hair. After combing her hair for two-three times, she hunts for lice with her fingers. If she finds either a louse or nit, she swats it with the help of the nail of her thumbs.

'...didn't get time to inform anyone. Actually speaking, it didn't strike me to inform anyone...'

A fellow sitting near us catches my eye and starts staring at me in an inquisitive manner. Tai sees him looking and asks, 'Do you recognize him? He is my cousin, Satish. Haven't you met him earlier?'

He gives a smile and says, 'I think so...I must have seen him. But I don't remember when and where.'

Tai nods at me and says, 'He is my younger brother-in-law. He stays at Nandgaon. I think you had met him when you came for our house-warming function.'

'Oh yes, yes.' He stops scratching his neck. 'I remember. I think you had come for an interview. Yes, right, I remember!'

'Had we met at that time?' I wondered aloud. Actually speaking, I don't remember anything.

'So what are you doing?' He asks me. Tai's attention is diverted to my niece, Pinky. She is still combing her hair. 'Why don't you comb your hair every day? Will you please sit properly? Why is that every now and then you are lifting your head?'

I give measured answers to his questions. He starts digging his ears. Pappu turns a page. Pinky sits with her head down. The mother of the two children is looking at the comb which is moving up and down the hair. I sit uncomfortably.

The children continue to have fun. The little girl hides under the sofa. He asks with his eyes closed, 'Ready?' She says 'Yes.' He takes his hands off from his eyes and looks here and there. I am still uncomfortable. He peeks under the sofa and screams 'Out…out!' Climbs on the sofa. Jumps. Dances. Then they swap and she closes her eyes. He looks around for a place to hide. He suddenly makes up his mind and goes and hides behind his mom. His mother tries to cover him with the edge of her sari.

I keep on looking uneasily.

'Has Dadasahib gone out somewhere?'

'Yes. In fact he told me he would be back soon but it's quite late already. Many people have come to pay a visit. Don't

180

worry, he'll be back. Enough of combing now!'

'Ready?' the little girl asks and lifts her head from the sofa. She looks around and asks her dad with body language. But his attention is not towards her.

'In a way, it is good that she passed away. She was already quite aged. Thank goodness, she has obtained emancipation! What was the point in being bedridden? As it is for the last five-six years, her memory was not supporting her. Poor thing, she has obtained emancipation,' Tai must have told this at least twice.

She pushes Pinky a bit and makes her get up. Patting down her hair, she looks at me, smiles and goes inside. That small girl has not found her brother. She calls out, 'Dada (elder brother)…'

He screams back 'Yyeess?' and gets caught. She pounces on him. Everyone, including Tai, laughs loudly, especially her brother-in-law. I try to control my laughter. When you are hiding, is there any need to answer if someone calls? More than him his mother feels bad. Their game starts again.

Tai collects the tangle of hair that has fallen on her sari and on the floor and rolls it with her fingers. 'Pappu is having his exams! What to do?'

'Oh is that so? When is it?' I ask for the heck of it.

'Pappu…!'

He unhappily lifts his head.

'When are your exams?'

'From the fifteenth,' he replies and thrusts his head back into the book, shaking his legs.

181

The servant who had opened the door for me approaches and asks, 'Madam, how much rice to cook?'

'You look around and decide. I am not hungry.'

'Even I am not hungry. Children have already eaten just now. What about you?'

That fellow near me wakes up.

'Need to cook rice. So I am asking. How hungry are you?'

'Not much. Throughout I have been sitting…' Yawns.

'You also have a little bit of rice. By that time he will come.' I am not attentive and engrossed looking at the children. I suddenly realize she is asking me.

'No, thank you. I have got some work. So need to leave.'

'How come every time you have some work or the other?' My eyes fall on the clock. Pappu throws down his book and goes inside. Pinky comes out. That fellow gets up and browses through a magazine.

I really ought to leave but my brother-in-law is yet to come.

The little boy suddenly starts crying. Everyone's attention goes towards him. Pappu comes out and goes to the record player. He is about to open the lid when he looks at Tai and again reclines on the sofa.

'Though she is small, she is very naughty,' says the mother, draws the boy close to her and pats him, 'And why are you crying like a girl?'

I become more uncomfortable. I must leave now. The mother pulls her son closer and gives him a peck on the cheeks. He tries to run away from her arms.

How come he has not yet come? I feel like telling her that I need to leave but don't have the courage to say so. It is said that it's not good to say that 'I'm leaving'. And at the same time it would look improper to get up all of a sudden and leave without saying anything. But leave I must. There is no point in waiting.

Whenever his brother-in-law, Tai's husband would return home, his mother would look at him intently and ask, 'Have you come?' He would say, 'Yes' and she would hover around him.

'Why were you so late?' She would ask.

'I got very busy with some work.'

'Now I suppose you won't be leaving.'

'No.'

'Did you have anything? Please eat my dear.' She would ask this question at any time of the day. If there were any guests in the room or any other person who was sitting with him for a long time, she would ask them also, 'Did you have anything?' No matter whether the answer was 'yes' or 'no', she would say, 'Please have something and then go, dear. Don't leave without eating.'

If her son got ready to go out anywhere, she would become restless. She would repeatedly ask, 'Are you going out anywhere, dear?'

He would answer, 'Yes'.

'Will you try to return early?'

'Yes.'

When he would be wearing his socks sitting on the sofa,

183

she would go and sit next to him. 'Oh dear! Please do come home early. Don't be too late.' After tying his shoelaces and rubbing his hands, she would put her arms around his neck. He would bend down and she would give a peck on his cheeks. Exactly like the one given by the mother to her little son some time ago. Whoever saw it for the first time would probably feel awkward. They, mother and son, didn't mind doing so. They behaved the same to each other whether they were alone or had an outsider near them. It didn't make any difference to them. I have also never seen him hurting her anytime by uttering something she wouldn't like. Even if a visitor was there, he never asked her to go and sit inside in an inner room.

I realized I was getting bored. I can't believe that such a lively house has become so dull, with a silence that seemed purposeful and long-drawn.

Tai gets up and adjusts her sari. The children are playing quietly now. That fellow gets up and goes to the window. Pappu comes and sits in the chair next to me. On his way, he picks up the newspaper that fellow has thrown. After browsing through the first page, he turns to the next page to read the advertisements of the cinema. I am bored.

'Okay, then…'

'Aren't you waiting?'

That fellow again sits in his place.

'Aunty, is it as hot in your area as it is here?' Pappu asks the lady on the sofa.

'It's okay, dear. You can leave. I can't guarantee when he

will be back,' Tai told me. She had picked up the word 'dear' from her mother-in-law. The style of talking was also the same.

I get up looking at that fellow. Tai is looking at me – for a long time. Even if she is not saying anything aloud, I feel she is telling me the same thing, 'Good that she passed away! Was already an aged person. Thank goodness, she has got emancipation! What was the point in living bedridden? As it is for last five-six years her memory was not supporting her. Poor thing, she has got emancipation!'

Aloud she said, 'Her death did not come as a shock. She was already aged. She wasn't well too. So in a way it is good that she is no more.' Why is she going on telling the same thing every now and then? Does she talk in the same way in front of her husband also? She was his mother. After her death he must have become more sensitive. What must he be undergoing listening to her insane talk? Knowing him, he must be ignoring her as usual.

I feel like meeting him but can't wait any more. It was clearly visible that my presence is disturbing everyone. To repeat the same things to everyone who comes to pay a visit is…When I get up, I sense the ease in the environment.

I walk to the door and wear my sandals. Except the two children, everyone is looking at me. Pappu gets up and comes to the door. He has come to close it after I leave. I pull the door to open it. If the door is not locked from inside, it keeps on banging.

Tai has already turned her back. Pinky has come out with

her hair tied up in a bun. Outside it is very bright. I realize that inside the house the tube light was not switched on.

Climbing down the steps, I heave a sigh of relief. The old lady's memories remain – especially of the empty cup and saucer and putting a peck on her son's cheek. How many times she must have told me, 'Please have something before leaving. Don't go without eating.'

As I get out of the society's gate, I stop as if I have stumbled over something. I see him coming. I am so much into my own world that I realize it only after he passes me by. He doesn't seem to recognize me; or else he would have stopped. I pause and keep looking at his rear as he walks ahead to his home. I don't wish to go back again to that house. Tai would definitely inform him that I had come.

Bus Ticket

H<small>E HAS BEEN WAITING</small> at the bus stop for quite some time. He was on his way to office. Buses simply rushed by, braked a little ahead of the stop, dropped a few people off and left without picking up passengers. Only one or two of those who sprinted towards the bus could clamber into it before it sped away, prompting the others to come back to where they were waiting at the bus stop. If buses stopped adjacent to the kerb, it invited the waiting passengers to storm in like a herd. Clambering into a bus requires supreme athleticism, great agility and the brute strength of a wrestler. Even if you do not have these attributes, you will soon acquire them once bus rides become a routine.

Even the most seasoned commuter will not be able to pinpoint who pushed him or her down. Sharp elbows and stomping feet are the weapons for furrowing one's way into a bus. You really cannot blame anyone if you hurt your ribs or stumble and fall. 'Better stay away and wait for another bus,' Babanrao reminded himself.

Babanrao has been in this city for many years, but he is still in awe of its complex undercurrents. He came here after passing the standard VII examination at his village school. Like most village youth, he came in search of a job. The amazing multiplicities of the city offered so much – some things he could understand, but much was beyond comprehension. The slow-moving tram always delighted him. He often wondered how a bus loaded with people could move on small tracks on the road with the help of overhead wires. But they had become fossils now and no longer trundled around in the city.

Like an octopus the city had grown over the years and the overburdened transport system was about to collapse. Yet people kept on commuting and underwent hazardous journeys to reach the city from the far-flung suburbs and returned home at night using local trains, buses, taxis, chasing the accelerating trains on slippery platforms, desperately clinging on to window frames of the compartment with fierce winds and wicked pylons slicing you, swaying on doorways with heels stuck precariously on footboards or sitting like a king on the top of a rake and playing Russian roulette with overhead high voltage wires. Babanrao never ever travelled on the footboard of a local train, not even when there was enough space to enjoy the crisp early morning breeze gushing through the door.

Don't these die-hards recklessly invite death every day? Or is it that they are ready to die? Are they inviting death by suicide? Questions float through Babanrao's pedantic mind and he broods on these life-and-death issues during his travels to and from work.

He is full of energy when he leaves home and after travelling for one hour in a crowded train and then walking for about 15 minutes, he reaches his office building. The return journey is not so easy. He hates his backward trip and is surprised as to why people hurry when homeward bound, especially during the evening peak-hour rush. As he reluctantly walks towards the subway which takes him to the central train station, one question keeps niggling him – why are people in an undue haste to reach home? What are they running away from? What is the urgency to catch, say, the 6:15 p.m. fast local? He cannot comprehend the paradox: why do people rush to travel through a transport system that is hell on wheels? Are they rushing home or are they running away from work? He keeps wondering at this conundrum to no answer.

While waiting for his bus, his favourite game is to watch faces and think about these nondescript dots. Suppose they reach ten-fifteen minutes late, is it going to make any drastic change? Is the wife or children or husband going to disappear? Why can't they read the newspapers which scream daily about terrible accidents – death while crossing a railway track or by falling off a speeding train, head banged by an electric pole, death by electrocution while traveling on top of the coach, crushed to death by a speeding motor car...Are these horror stories not enough to scare away people from crossing roads on a red signal or rushing to the station to catch running trains or travelling by bus on the edge of the door or hanging on to a steel bar near the doorway without a proper foothold? One look at people crossing roads convinces him that news stories warning pedestrians are not enough to scare them. Babanrao cannot help feeling dejected by what he sees and reads. A couple of years ago, he was unwell and bedridden for almost six months, and developed this habit of thinking too much about too many things.

At times he wonders how he can think so clearly about so many things in one go and pities others who do not think and live their lives like cattle. The sight of people rushing towards the suburban train station is like a herd of cows and bullocks returning to their stables at sundown every day. The animals however amble their way back home while human beings rush back in a frenzy.

Babanrao never rushes, and takes pride in slowly marching towards the railway station like a victorious warrior. He has some self-imposed rules for daily train journeys: no hanging out of a running train, no travelling on footboard, no catching a running train. It's not possible for him to practice these things now but even when it was possible a couple of years ago, he never thought of doing them. He never got into a running train or alighted from one. Nor did he ever board a bus with a milling and chaotic crowd. He distanced himself from the madness of ever-increasing commuters.

The difference between getting into a fast train and missing one is a matter of ten-fifteen minutes. So why risk life and limb – he asks himself and others who try to cajole him into boarding a train in this frenzied manner. How 'not to risk a life for saving ten-fifteen minutes' is his pet sermon and he is willing to talk and elaborate on this to anybody including strangers waiting for a bus or a train. He begins his conversations with strangers by exclaiming 'What the hell do these guys think of themselves? Are they Tarzans or circus artists?' He then goes on to explain why it is risky to join such a mad rush. But he has stopped expounding on this subject in his office since he had talked about it so often in the past that he is sure it has become a big joke with his colleagues.

His colleagues who reside near him in the suburbs have a consensus: if they travel with Babanrao, they will have a hassle-free journey. He knows which bus arrives when and which train will be crowded on which day. He anticipates which train will start from which platform and is usually right about train timings.

He reaches office mostly on time. If there is any trouble, he informs office and takes a casual leave from work. And when he does arrive late for work, he is not questioned. 'Surely there must have been some traffic problem. Babanrao is a simple, trustworthy man,' his General Manager had once said in front of the entire office when he was late. And sure enough, he had got late due to the derailment of a train. Babanrao had never taken any undue advantage of this trust shown by the manager by coming late and blaming traffic jams.

His wife worries about his habit of getting lost in his own thoughts. Waiting at the bus stop, he becomes so engrossed in his world that he is oblivious to the various sounds and movements around him. When he starts thinking, it is like shutting a door. He enjoys this temporary detachment, this peace amidst the chaos and noise pollution around him.

He doesn't realize when the bus arrives, stops in front of him and he is pushed inside. He has already boarded the bus. He is pushed to one side where he tries to hold on to the safety bar over his head and holds on to his briefcase in the other hand.

He is crushed from all four sides as he tries to move further along the crowded aisle in the bus. Someone stamps on his foot. No seat is available and he has to stand in the aisle. He tries to keep his balance by clutching the safety bar and holding his briefcase. The conductor shouts 'Move ahead' and jerks at an overhead string attached to a warning bell. The bus starts abruptly and as the standing passengers sway, Babanrao loses his balance. Despite this, he doesn't fall as he is kept upright by the crowd tightly packed around him. A boy standing just behind falls all over him, making it difficult for Babanrao to regain his former position.

The conductor now yells 'Ticket, ticket' and makes a clicking noise with a handheld ticket-punching machine. A perspiring Babanrao can feel the conductor's presence behind him but cannot turn.

Clutching the briefcase between his two legs and keeping a tight grip on the safety bar above his head, he tries to take out some loose change from his trouser pocket. The bus stops with a jerk and Babanrao's head bumps into someone else's. The conductor is shouting and discouraging passengers from boarding the bus that is already chock-full of people and yells at the driver to move on. Babanrao moves a few steps forward as a few commuters get down quickly. Before he can get into a vacant seat in front of him, someone more alert and forceful rushes past from behind him and occupies the seat.

Everyone settles down as the bus moves on to the next stop, the conductor edges closer to him. He tries to take out the change from his trouser pocket but gives up as he cannot keep his balance. Meanwhile, he notices someone nearby is ready to get down. This time Babanrao positions himself well and lowers himself down onto the seat just as the fellow gets up to go. Much relieved, he places his briefcase on his lap; takes out his handkerchief, which is a very difficult exercise as he is cramped from all sides and wipes sweat from his face and forehead. His elbow hurts the person sitting next to him but he does not say anything. Babanrao nods apologetically. He feels very weak and exhausted.

The bus stops and there is a lot of jostling with some commuters getting on and others getting off. But it's no longer a matter of concern for Babanrao as now he has got a seat. As the conductor comes up to him, he tries to take out some change but finds it difficult as it is at the bottom of a pocket that is stuffed with a small diary, pass holder, some receipts and a few folded notepapers. He takes them all out one by one and puts them back in his shirt pocket before taking out one ten-rupee note and holding it in front of the conductor. But the conductor is busy counting the loose change given by another commuter and ignores Babanrao.

Babanrao keeps holding the note in his hand, waiting for the conductor to take his money and give a bus ticket in return. The conductor appears to be young, has grown his hair long and keeps a cap reluctantly on his head, which gives him a comical look. He is holding a tin box with a series of tickets and a leather money-bag, both of which are attached to long leather belts. It requires great skill to hold both the bags, punch out tickets, take money and return the change. He appears to be grumpy and not used to conducting this balancing act. He stops giving tickets when the bus takes a turn and he can't hold himself straight.

The conductor frowns when he sees the ten-rupee note in Babanrao's hand.

'Where to?'

'Mantralaya.'

He pushes the note into the back pocket of his money-bag. Takes out change, opens the cover of the tin bag, yanks out one ticket, punches it and hands it over along with change to Babanrao without looking at him.

Babanrao takes the ticket first and holds his hand out for the change. The conductor hands over the ticket and the change simultaneously. One coin rolls down, two fall on his lap and one remains in his palm.

'Hold the change properly. You should not give currency notes during peak hours…moreover, you can't even hold coins properly,' remarks the conductor, moving on, without waiting for Babanrao to collect his coins.

Babanrao bends down and collects two ten-paise coins, someone hands him a five-rupee coin from behind. He continues to look around, not knowing whether there are any more to collect.

'Got everything?' the conductor shouts as he gives tickets to other passengers.

'Five rupees seventy paise, a five-paise coin is missing. Anyway, it's okay,' says Babanrao in a weak voice.

Babanrao continues his search for the remaining five paise. One elderly person is watching all this tamasha (drama) over coins.

'Just move your foot, not this one the other one, yes, it's just below it, that's right,' he directs Babanrao as he recovers his last five-paise coin.

Babanrao closes his eyes. He is tired and does not want to look at the crowd around him.

He wakes up as the person sitting near the window shuffles and gets ready to get up. The last stop has come. The bus takes a long turn and shudders to a halt with a screeching sound. The driver gets off. Everyone is in a hurry to get down. As the commuters get off the bus, Babanrao peeps out while moving forward. He notices a ticket checker in a white dress and black cap asking for tickets from commuters, 'Why should he come now, at peak hour?' someone grumbles loudly.

As he approaches the door, Babanrao recollects a pile of files waiting for him on his office desk. He puts his hand in his shirt pocket for the bus ticket as he alights with briefcase in the other. The chubby-faced ticket checker looks nonchalantly at the bus commuters through his thick glasses. He is impatient with those who take more time to show their ticket. Babanrao alights and moves a little away to allow others to get down as his fingers do not find the ticket in his shirt pocket. He puts his bag down and checks his shirt pocket. It's empty. Impossible! Where is the ticket? – he asks himself.

The conductor asks him to stand a little away as he has become an obstacle for others. The checker is busy with other passengers. Babanrao places his bag near his legs and starts searching through the right pocket of his trousers. Handkerchief, office keys, house keys, diary, he takes them out and ensures that ticket is not in the right pocket and puts everything back. Then starts with the left pocket, finds some receipts, papers, and the change just collected from conductor but no bus ticket.

Where has it gone? By now Babanrao has become nervous. Almost everyone has alighted. The conductor and checker walk up to him. The conductor has removed his cap and is holding it in his hand. Babanrao is sweating. He has checked through all his pockets but there is no trace of the ticket. A big crowd has gathered around him. He perspires even more. The crowd includes some of those who had travelled with him. One teenager smiles sheepishly making him more nervous.

He feels guilty and nervous.

The conductor and checker are waiting for him. Both are irritated by the delay. The driver now joins them.

'What's the matter, can't find the ticket?' The driver is sympathetic.

'No, I don't know where it has gone,' he says and begins a second search of his pockets.

'Good catch…cheaters!' someone remarks. Babanrao realizes the spot of trouble he is in. He begins to tremble. His throat is suddenly dry and he feels as if he cannot speak. He is a law-abiding citizen who has never been confronted by a policeman, ticket checker or municipal tax collector. He is very punctual in paying dues to the government and other bodies and cannot imagine travelling without ticket. He feels ashamed. Now unless he finds the ticket, no one will ever believe that he had purchased it in its first place.

Will I find the ticket or not? He keeps on thinking quickly. Let me tell the checker that I had purchased a ticket but cannot find it in my pocket. Might have dropped it or misplaced it somewhere. If he does not accept my plea, I will pay the fine. He felt like screaming and telling them that he had no intention of travelling without ticket. But he can't utter a word. He feels like a petty criminal waiting for police to take him into custody.

It has never happened before. He has never lost a ticket.

He would always fold it and keep it in his shirt pocket. He would even fold it in such a manner that it could be easily retrieved from the pocket. This is second nature with Babanrao…Once he gets a ticket, he automatically folds it and slips it into his shirt pocket without any delay so there is no question of it going here or there. It has become a matter of habit for him to preserve the ticket till he reaches office.

'Where is the ticket?' The checker is losing his patience. He spits out tobacco juice. Babanrao mumbles something and keeps on checking things in his pocket.

'Have you dropped it in the bus?' asks the driver and enters the bus from the front and Babanrao follows him. They look for a ticket below the seat where he was sitting but there's no sign of the ticket. The checker spits once again when he sees both getting down from the bus empty-handed.

Babanrao now hopes that no one from his office is watching this tamasha…

'It's not there,' says the checker in an accusatory tone.

'Brother, I checked everywhere, it's not there.'

'Okay, I can't wait any longer. But had you really purchased one?' the checker asks without looking at him. He takes out a receipt book for imposing a penalty for travelling without ticket.

Babanrao is furious at the checker's accusation. How could anyone think that he had been travelling without a ticket? He began trembling with rage.

'Is it a crime to lose a ticket? If not, then take your penalty and let me go. But I want to make it clear that I did not travel without ticket.' But these words don't find an expression. They remain in his mind. Babanrao cannot open his mouth and utter a single word. He is hoping that the conductor would support his claim that he has purchased his ticket, but the conductor is nowhere near him; he has walked away.

'What are you looking at? Get lost, this is no circus,' the checker shouts at the street urchins waiting to see what is happening to the potbellied, middle-aged man. The other commuters have left. The urchins walk away but they keep on playing at the other end of the fence.

'How long should we stand below this hot sun? Let's stand below some shade. Check for the last time whether you have the ticket or not, or else pay the fine.' The checker moves ahead, followed by Babanrao and the driver.

They enter a box-like wooden cabin which serves as a temporary office. Babanrao put his bag down. He is now feeling a little relieved that no one is looking at him. He begins the third and final search of his pockets mumbling, 'I travelled for so many years but never lost a ticket.' No one is interested in what he is saying. They all want to see the ticket.

He pours the entire contents of his right pocket of his trouser on the small table and looks at each and every thing closely. He unfolds the handkerchief and flutters it open to see if it has got stuck somewhere. While taking out his handkerchief, he sees the conductor coming in. Gesturing at him, he says, 'I had purchased a ticket. If you want, you can ask him.'

The conductor does not look at him but says, 'There are so

many passengers travelling daily. How do I remember all of them? It is your responsibility to retain the ticket.'

There is no expression on the checker's face. Babanrao does not know whether the checker is even listening to what he is saying but he persists with the conductor.

'I know you cannot remember everyone, but you can certainly remember me. I dropped the change on the floor ...you recall?'

There is no response and no one is interested to find out whether he has purchased a ticket or not. He puts the things back into his right pocket and begins taking out a diary and some papers from the left one.

'See Mister, where do you work?'

'Vishal Construction Company. Why?'

'It is not a question of whether you purchased the ticket or not but whether you have it with you now. If you have it, show it, and if you cannot show it then legally speaking you have travelled without ticket and you will be penalized accordingly. You pay the penalty and get going. No one has time to waste.'

Babanrao doesn't say anything. He simply checks and empties everything on the table – change, electricity bill, friend's letter, an application addressed to the municipal corporation. He unfolds all these papers with the hope that the ticket would pop up from somewhere. He starts putting back all the things one by one and the diary is the last thing he picks up from the table. There are only currency notes. The moment he takes them out in his hand, the neatly folded ticket falls on the floor. How did it go inside the diary? He does not say anything, simply bends to pick it and hands it over to the checker without any expression on his face.

The checker punches it and gives it back. The driver who has been sympathetic says, 'See we knew you must have kept it somewhere.' Babanrao doesn't respond. The entire exercise has numbed him.

'You keep the ticket in one place and search somewhere else. How will you find it?' The driver heaves a sigh of relief as if it was his ticket that had got lost. 'It's okay. Be careful from next time,' he says.

Babanrao is angry with himself. How can he be so casual about the ticket? He wipes the sweat on his face, lifts his bag and moves out. The conductor is busy giving his account while the checker is busy completing his paperwork. No one takes any heed of his exit. After getting out of that box-like cabin he pauses to heave a sigh of relief.

He slowly moves towards a small lane to his office. The urchins who were driven away from near the cabin are still playing at the corner. They smile at him to show him that they knew what happened. One boy slinging a cricket bat shouts, 'They have set him free!' Every one laughs. This must be their routine fun spot!

With their laughter, his short-term satisfaction at finding the ticket disappears. Ignoring those kids, he starts walking briskly towards the office building. His steps slow down as he wonders whether or not anyone from the office witnessed the drama at the bus stop.

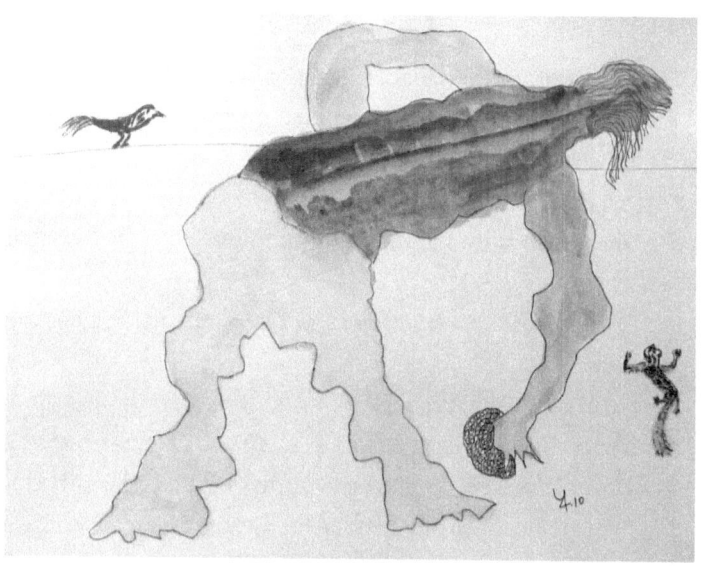

Speaking with Sparrows

H E TURNED ON THE TAP. No water came out, instead, ffaasshh ffuusshh sounds could be heard for a long time. A few drops dripped down from the nozzle after a while.

Thinking that today too he would have to go down to fetch water, he turned back from the terrace.

One could hear All India Radio play at a low volume somewhere. When it was not on, an eerie ssuuuiiiinnnngg sound began humming in his head. When the radio was on, at least there was some relief from the unidentified clamour sounding at the back of the ears. Moreover, it helps to distract from the dead silence.

The morning newspaper had not yet come. He could not predict when it would. It depended on the arrival of the bus. So, he decided to take a bath.

'Sir…'

'Yes? Who is it?' He turned back to see who it was. No one was there.

A cold breeze was blowing. The shevanti leaves were swaying.

He entered the kitchen.

'Stored water gets heated faster. But heating is an additional problem. Life in Pune was better. Twenty-four hours' water supply plus geyser for heating water. What can be done? You wanted to stay near nature – now you have it!'

He boiled some water in a vessel and poured it into a bucket and entered the bathroom.

It was better to bathe before Shanta came in. Once she started sweeping and mopping, one had to shuttle from one room to the other.

She knocked on the door. He had told her umpteen times not to knock. But it was difficult for her to reach the bell. And even if her hand somehow reached the bell and she tried to ring it, it was not audible. To add to that, most of the time there was no power supply, so she preferred knocking on the door.

There was one good thing about her though. Immediately after entering the house, she first headed towards the bathroom and washed her hands and feet. And gosh! The way she went about her work! It was at such a high speed that it seemed she just wanted to finish it really fast and then leave the house.

'Baba, which bhaji (vegetable) should I cook?' she asked every day without fail.

'See if any vegetable is left. I will get some in the evening if there is nothing,' was his staple answer.

Shanta called him Baba, so the entire village had also started calling him that.

Only the people from the terrace called him 'Sir'. God knows who taught them that! They might be addressing him thus out of habit.

Since it was a new place for him, a countryside village, he hardly knew anyone. When he had come to live here five years ago, there was not much activity in this sleepy village. This village and the town nearby were separated by a huge moorland. But these days, it was gradually shrinking. Actually, the distance was the same, but since the population had increased, it looked as though it had come closer. Instead of having to depend entirely on the bus service, he could hop on to a rickshaw. And the small town didn't seem to be very far.

After taking a bath, he joined his hands. That was the only way he offered prayers. Earlier, there used to be no sacred objects or idols of any god in his house. During her first visit to his village house, his younger sister, Akka, had admonished him for not having any idols in the house. She insisted that he must have at least a small idol of a crawling young Lord Krishna and the Goddess Amba, made of brass. Ultimately, she herself bought them and convinced him to fold his hands at least once a day after taking a bath.

No one had liked the idea of his going and staying in such a secluded village. He remained adamant. His son had settled in Australia long ago. His wife had died a sudden death. No one had expected her to die from a mere fever that gradually turned fatal. He left Pune. He did not listen to anyone. His sister then asked, 'Who will look after you? You don't know anyone there.' But he never bothered to reply to her.

His son had called up before he left Pune. When his mother died, he came and stayed for some ten days. He had brought his wife along with him. The son couldn't wait for the last rites on the twelfth and thirteenth days. But he was satisfied that at least his son had come.

In spite of ardent requests to stay back, his son had left for Australia along with his wife. Somehow, he held his son responsible for his mother's declining health. When he left for Australia despite her opposition, she felt dejected and her health problems got complicated with the passing days.

Every now and then, she used to plead with him, 'Please call up our son, please call up our son.' And he used to avoid the issue saying, 'My pension money will get over. Why doesn't he call up?'

Before leaving, his son had told him, 'Baba, instead of staying here all alone, come along with me. All facilities are available in Australia. And for whom are you going to stay here?'

'For whom?' He didn't say anything. 'Let's see some other

time.' He avoided giving him any clear answer.

After his son left, Akka stayed on for four days. Then even she left. He felt lonely and desolate.

He had decided to give away all the gold and silver ornaments to his daughter-in-law. But Akka advised him to have patience. 'Oh dear, you can give them to her later; she will surely come back again.' So he kept aside the ornaments at Akka's insistence.

'Dada, why don't you stay with Manu?'

'What am I going to do there? For the initial two or three days, it would be okay. But what next? What's wrong with staying here? And even all of you are here.'

'Yeah, I know. But your daughter-in-law has conceived.'

'So? What am I going to do? Help her into her puerperal state? And I didn't know that she has conceived.'

'No, no. In fact, you will be good company for your children. When you bluntly said "No", your son felt a bit uncomfortable and awkward.'

'We had not agreed with their decision to go and settle there. But since they had already decided, what could we do? It was not possible to hold them back. It's okay. Let it be. As of now, I cannot go. Let's see later.' The topic was left hanging.

Manu had told her, 'What's wrong if he comes for five-six months. Of what use is he, otherwise?' She didn't say anything. But she had felt a bit queer. She wanted to say something, but kept mum. Why aggravate the strained relationship between father and son and spoil it!

His son left. He didn't go. It was difficult passing the time alone. How many times could he go and sit at the Shani temple? The same old people and the same old topics! They kept enquiring about each other's health. He was disgusted with everything that transpired there.

Somehow, he managed to put up with the situation, but then decided to introduce a change. Most of his friends had dispersed. Some had gone to live with their sons. Others who didn't have sons had gone to live with their daughters. Some had left the city. Earlier, people used to come to live in Pune after retirement, but now it was the other way round.

After two or three knocks on the door, he came back to his senses. He walked briskly to unbolt it.

There was no need to latch the door, because apart from him, there was no one who would come. And he had nowhere to go. So there was a simple bolt which just had to be turned around and pulled down and the door would open.

When the door opened, there was no one there. Maybe he had been hallucinating about the knock on the door.

This morning, from the moment he had sat down for his meditation, every now and then he had found himself remembering the countryside well. He wondered why this was so.

But when he actually started chanting god's name with the help of the rosary beads, he felt a little better. After fifteen to twenty minutes, he felt his mind had calmed down.

His guru had told him, 'When you are chanting the name of god with the help of rosary beads, try to concentrate in such a way that no other thought should penetrate your mind. It will be difficult initially, but try it out. It will be possible, but gradually.'

Sometimes it was possible. But sometimes it wasn't.

He looked at his toe. It was completely swollen due to pus. His toe had banged against the washing machine. But he hadn't imagined that water would become the reason for such a painful infection.

Forget about the mind – concentrating or becoming impassive. Every now and then, his attention was being diverted to that painful toe. When he was young and lived in the countryside, his toe had got swollen in the same manner. It hadn't got infected with pus, but half of the nail of the big toe had got torn off. He had dived into the well, but by mistake, had gone closer towards the opposite wall. And had bruised the big toe against a stone that was jutting out of it. Only when he was out of the well did he realize that the nail had got torn off.

Blood had got clotted and the nail torn off. Unbearable pain. Countryside well. Painful toe, unsteady, diverted mind…

As you close your eyes and concentrate on the middle of the two eyebrows, you start seeing a red ball, which has four corners of darkness.

Why was the mind getting diverted towards other parts of the body? Memories from the past were hounding him.

He opened a container kept in a corner. He took out some grains of muesli that were wrapped in a silver foil. Poured them into a cup. He poured milk into the cup. Since it was burning hot, he needed to keep it aside for some more time. He covered it with a saucer. Went to the hall. He had already read yesterday's paper. Still, he was searching for any unread news. Unnecessarily, he read the newspaper again and again. He was very hungry. He went in again, took the cup and started eating with a spoon. 'What's this muesli-fuesli? Eating the same thing every day that resembles animal fodder. Buffaloes are fed this. But who is going to cook bhaji and roti early morning? Obviously, one has to eat something like this – sealed and packed.'

There was a cook, but she came late.

'Is she going to come early for you?' Someone spoke from the terrace. But he ignored it. He picked up the last two-three grains with the spoon and put them in his mouth. Washed the cup under running water, else it became difficult to clean. He fetched a medicine bottle that was kept on the plank and took out a strip of tablets. Out of twelve, eight were over. He needed to take one tablet a day. The doctor had warned him not to forget the medicine. Must take one. BP is fluctuating every now and then.

'Oh doctor, why should I have high BP? My wife is no more and my son has gone abroad and is quite happily settled there. Then why this vexatious matter?'

'Look, it's unpredictable. It's not in our hands. If one's weight increases, it can be reduced. If one's sugar increases, it can be reduced. But if one's BP increases, nothing can be done. It enters straight into your brain, and then just nothing can be done. Instead, take one tablet every day.'

He had said, 'Yes doctor,' and had started taking one tablet every day, without fail.

When he was taking the tablets out of the foil, one fell down. 'What's the use now?' He took out another one and gulped it down with water. Picked up the one that had fallen and threw it out of the window, towards the mountain.

'At least the mountain's BP will get lowered!' he said to himself and giggled. She never used to like such poor jokes.

'Wow, nice tablet.'

Without even looking back, he caught on that the squirrel had spoken.

'I didn't throw it to you. Your head will unnecessarily start spinning.'

'It's okay. Let it spin.'

'Let it spin! Then let it spin. What have I got to do with it?'

He opened a bottle and put a date into his mouth. He took out the seed and washed it. 'Now what to do? If I throw it in the dustbin, it will go waste. There are so many mountains around.' He took the seed and went to the terrace. Greenery was swaying over it. That was the reason he had left the city and come to the countryside village. 'But in summer, everything becomes arid. The trees and grass dry up. The land looks parched. But now, look, how lush green it is!' He felt happy being with nature.

'Is the jungle outside going to shrink inwards? Branches have already started penetrating in.' So an iron grill was fixed on the terrace. He put that seed on the wall of the balcony and jettisoned it forward with the help of his thumb and middle finger, as though pushing the striker of a carrom board. If he had hurled it with his hand instead, there were chances that it would have collided with the grill.

He did not know where the seed had fallen. But it must have crossed the building's yard and fallen on the other side.

Smiling at himself, he went inside. Now a date tree was going to grow on the other side.

'Oh dear! Do you think that hurling a seed will make a tree grow? And that, too, of dates?'

Who said that? No one could be seen on the terrace. 'It must definitely be the porcupine,' he thought. 'No one talks with me, but at least these people talk. Some amusement.'

He walked back in. But what sort of meditation was he going to do? He thought that after taking a bath, he would wait for the newspaper. So he went in to search for his towel.

'Can't predict where it must have been hung for drying. She has been told umpteen times to dry it in a particular place, so that there is no need to search for it every morning. But she never remembers this. Or it might be something unimportant, according to her.'

'What are you searching for?'

'Nothing. What have you got to do with it?'

'Towel?'

'Yes.'

'It's right behind you; hung on the yoke-pin.'

'Oh, how did I not realize that?'

'Is something bothering you these days? Then why didn't you see it?'

'Just shut up, don't be nosy.'

'Oh god! These people have started talking too much.' Speaking to himself, he turned towards the bathroom.

But there was a knock again. Hanging the towel on his shoulder, he came out and opened the door.

She came in and straight away entered the bathroom. Washing her hands and legs, she took the broom that was kept behind the door and started sweeping at once.

While coming in, she had picked up the paper that was tucked on the door and put it on the chair. He picked it up. 'Now no worries at all for half an hour! I'll finish reading while she finishes her sweeping and mopping. These days there's nothing much to read,' he told himself.

'Oh, is that so sir? Then why do you buy a newspaper? Stop buying it,' the squirrel from the terrace told him.

'You think you're too smart.' He got annoyed.

'Then what should I do?'

'Just shut up. These days you have become too nosy.'

By the time he finished reading the newspaper, she had finished doing all her work. As usual, while closing the door behind her, she said loudly, 'I'm leaving' and left. He dragged the towel, which he had hung off his shoulder, onto his thigh.

He was feeling a bit lazy. 'Whether I bathe or not, what difference is it going to make? Who is going to ask here? When I am hungry, obviously I will get up. My meal is ready.'

He lay down on the bed.

The reflection of the sun's rays was gradually withdrawing from the room. Since he saw the reflection of the sun's rays

213

every day, he had realized that their length and breadth and the way they exited changed every month. The sun's progress either to the north or to the south always takes place without our knowledge.

When he closed his eyes, a blood-red ball appeared under his closed eyelids. But as he was looking at it, the clamour on the terrace started increasing again. 'Has everyone started talking together? It is just getting impossible to understand who is saying what!'

Without moving, he kept lying on the bed.

The clamour in his head kept on increasing.

RATNA TRANSLATION SERIES

A Faceless Evening and other stories
by GANGADHAR GADGIL
Translated from Marathi by Keerti Ramachandra

'Gangadhar Gadgil's stories open up not a region and its people, but also a time. Keerti Ramachandra's translation is an important effort to know that place, people, and time.' – *National Herald*

'Keerti Ramachandra brings these complex tales to life through her translation. She captures the essence of each story.'
– *Muse India Journal*

'The images are interesting, unorthodox and reflect the Marathi sensibility through English translations very well.' – *Deccan Herald*

'Keerti Ramachandra…has maintained the essence of Gadgil's style. The book is a great treat for Gadgil fans and equally enchanting for introduction to an author who pioneered a new class of Marathi short stories.' – *Free Press Journal*

'Keerti Ramachandra has displayed exceptional skills in getting the essence of each story in the English version along with the tone of the writer.' – USHA TAMBE, *Writer*

'Keerti moves fluently in both languages with a creative mind; she can hear the inner voice of a writer. We enter the fascinating world of Gadgil's short stories and are left with the desire to read more.'
– SANIYA, *Writer*

The Story of Being Useless
&
Three Contexts of a Writer
by AVADHOOT DONGARE
Translated from Marathi by Nadeem Khan

'Avadhoot Dongare is a young promising Marathi novelist. He was awarded the Sahitya Akademi Yuva Puraskar, 2014, for his novella *Svatahala Faltu Samjanyachi Goshta* (The Story of Being Useless). He has a phenomenally different way of telling a story. In his novellas, the writer narrating the story is present. Once he starts telling the story, he moves out of the picture. The characters that he has created start behaving independently.

'The two novellas – *The Story of Being Useless* and *Three Contexts of a Writer* – are also about the act of writing novels. What the novelist writes is not true or false. It goes beyond this. The characters, events taking place in the novel are the creation of the novelist. However, they are entwined with real events. Reality and the writer's perspective merge. Avadhoot Dongare expresses our reality, the politics of living in our times through the stories of ordinary lives. His narration is simple, but subtle.

'These excellent translations, by Nadeem Khan, are a need of the times, enabling the stories to reach out to the world.'

VASANT ABAJI DAHAKE, *Poet and Critic*

RATNA TRANSLATION SERIES

The Song of Life and other stories
by VIJAYA RAJADHYAKSHA
Translated from Marathi by Keerti Ramachandra

One of the most senior women writers in Marathi, Vijaya Rajadhyaksha's short stories reflect the eternal human dilemma…the self versus society, ambition versus duty, choice versus compromise…Her protagonist is the successful urban educated woman who questions a man's capacity to understand her and wonders who is at fault…Her women talk to the reader through a series of agonizing introspections, until they come to terms with their physical, mental and spiritual selves. Reiterating eternal values of family, roots, bonds and ties, the stories showcase how lives are inextricably linked in the quest for peace, solace and fulfilment.

In three stories with male protagonists, the author portrays with sensitivity the conflicts and quandaries of a man's world. Whereas men have created strong women characters, it is rare to find a woman who has written so convincingly about her men.

RATNA TRANSLATION SERIES

Havan

– a novel –

by MALLIKARJUN HIREMATH

Translated from Kannada by S. Mohanraj

'Hiremath's novel and stories are based in the geographical and cultural surroundings of Bagalkote. The works closely describe the lives of different communities that live here, their struggles, different skills they have, vocations they pursue and their language and customs. Neither the localized environment nor the language seems to have imposed any restrictions on Hiremath's narratives. They become functional and cease to be ornamental. *Havan* documents the unique life pattern of a community and attracts the reader with its lucid narrative providing a perspective on human life…

'*Havan* is a novel that haunts us for a long time. It compels us to read and reread.'

T.P. ASHOK, *Critic*